SAVING LINCOLN

Published by
Saving Lincoln, LLC
5042 Wilshire Blvd. Suite 170
Los Angeles, CA 90036

Cover design by Yada Khoongumjorn
Front-cover art by Dan Chapman

Back-cover photo:
6th New York Artillery encampment
Brandy Station, VA, ca. 1864
Library of Congress

ISBN: 978-0-9894243-0-1

To the brave men who fought and died in the Civil War.

Foreword
by
Brooks D. Simpson

Ward Hill Lamon thought a great deal of himself. A Virginian by birth and a lawyer by training, he had little patience for meddlesome northerners who made it their business to do what they could to disrupt and even destroy the institution of slavery. Yet he soon found himself drawn to an Illinois lawyer who despised the peculiar institution, and who believed that it would one day imperil the continued existence of the American republic. That man, of course, was Abraham Lincoln, and *Saving Lincoln* is the story of a friendship between two very different men... and it is so much more.

Given his political preferences, it is something of a miracle that Lamon became Lincoln's steadfast friend, loyal at all costs, even when it cost him something. No one could have foreseen him becoming a Republican, and Lincoln could not see him becoming a diplomat, a position for which the blunt Lamon was clearly unsuited. However, the president-elect saw in Lamon someone he could trust, and asked him to come to Washington.

Lamon took it upon himself to keep Lincoln out of harm's way. This was no mean feat, for the sixteenth president often shrugged off talk about assassination threats, observing that if someone really wanted to kill him, the assassin would be successful. Lamon believed otherwise: in any case, it was not wise to tempt fate. He accompanied Lincoln as the president-elect made his way through Baltimore under cover of darkness to thwart one murderous plot; he was known to beat down with a single blow people who tried to inflict pain on the president while pretending to shake his hand. No stranger to feats of strength, Lincoln once suggested that Lamon refrain from hitting a would-be assailant with his fist, but to "strike him with a club or crowbar or something that won't kill him."

The president entrusted Lamon with several important tasks. He dispatched Lamon to South Carolina in the spring of 1861 to assess the strength of secessionist sentiment and to learn just how likely an outbreak of hostilities might be. Lamon may well have fumbled his task a bit, reportedly informing South Carolina governor Francis Pickens that the Lincoln administration was planning to withdraw from Fort Sumter just as Lincoln had decided to retain control of that installation in Charleston Harbor. Later, as marshal for the District of Columbia, Lamon proved a controversial figure. When he chose to enforce the Fugitive Slave Law, congressional Republicans sliced his salary, an act Lincoln chose not to veto. In acting as he did Lamon was supported by the president, who asserted that one had to enforce the laws on the books until Congress altered or repealed them. In November 1863 Lamon presided at the formal ceremonies for the dedication of a national military cemetery at Gettysburg, where he heard his friend deliver a few appropriate remarks.

In *Saving Lincoln*, Sal and Nina Litvak offer us a view of the many sides of the sixteenth president. We see someone who loved to tell a story, laugh, and even sing; a man who pondered fate and lapsed into what people then called melancholy, a deep sadness some suspect was depression; a man who loved his wife and sons and was shattered when his son Willie died in 1862. We view a president who was determined to win a war whatever the cost, even when that cost hit close to home in the form of friends and relatives falling at the front. We watch him wrestle with the responsibility that he keenly bore in waging that war and his evolving commitment to strike at slavery. In short, this is more than just a story of a friendship, although it is through the friendship that we often see Lincoln the president.

But the Lincoln Lamon knew is not the entire story of this film. Along the way we watch the fall of McClellan and the rise of Grant; we observe the wondrous ability of the press to twist, poke, prod, and distort; the many critics of the administration's policies from all angles, from those who thought he wasn't trying hard enough to those who urged him to pull back from escalating the conflict. We feel compassion for the often-mocked Mary Lincoln as she copes with Willie's death. Lamon did what he could to relieve the suffering around him, playing his banjo while singing a well-known ditty designed to bring a smile to Lincoln's face, although even that practice once led to newspaper criticism that Lincoln had sang and joked his way across Antietam battlefield as he passed the graves of fallen soldiers.

As a self-appointed bodyguard for the president, Lamon found his task a daunting one. It was one thing to smuggle a disguised president-elect through Baltimore in the dead of night, but Lincoln's disregard for his own personal safety became even more of a challenge once war broke out. Lamon did what he could to stay by his friend's side, although he struggled to prevent the president from testing fate (this is perhaps most visibly shown when Lincoln visited Fort Stevens in July 1864 to observe the Confederate attack on the outskirts of Washington ... even if in fact we don't know whether Lamon was present). Lamon himself tells us that in April 1865, when Lincoln dispatched him to Richmond, Lamon warned Lincoln to take better care of his own safety, and explicitly told him to avoid the theater.

The keen eye of the scholar and Civil War buff will doubtless discern places where a filmmaker's desire for drama or the demands of compressing and combining various events to fit within the tight confines of 101 minutes try the patience of those devoted to historical accuracy... at least as they define it. Yet one finds much more that is quite compelling, even with the artistic license that cultivates our imagination. Tom Amandes' portrayal of Lincoln is simply brilliant, bringing an icon to life in ways that make us appreciate his rich humanity. Lea Coco's memorable rendering of the blustering Lamon honors the president's loyal protector in suitable fashion, and does so with a light comic touch that is all too fitting. The dynamic between these two men, with Lincoln confiding in Lamon while his friend struggles with the challenges of protecting the president from others, and sometimes from himself, is convincingly captured in the movie.

Saving Lincoln manages to tell all of these stories, and it does so in ways that leave one smiling at one moment and deathly still the next. All the while one is painfully aware of the approaching climax, for, after all, we know what will happen. When, in the wake of Appomattox, Lincoln declares he can now dispense with Lamon's protection, he does so because Lamon has nothing more to protect: Lincoln has fulfilled the task for which he came to believe God had chosen him. Days later, it ends, just as Lamon had feared, with Lincoln at the theater, holding Mary's hand and enjoying a play when the curtain came down on his life. Yet it is not the least accomplishment of this film that in its own way it saves Lincoln by bringing him back to life as a man who loved, laughed, and enjoyed the company of one Ward Hill Lamon. Lincoln loved a good story, and what follows is one of the best in American history.

Introduction

A Film of, by and for the People
by
Salvador Litvak
Director, *Saving Lincoln*

     My "a-ha!" moment occurred late at night while sleuthing through the online Prints & Photographs Division of the Library of Congress. I stared at a high resolution image of a glass plate negative created in 1865. The photograph depicted wounded Union soldiers in an Army hospital. I zoomed deep into the picture and focused on an emaciated young soldier sitting at the back of the room. His eyes pierced mine, and I wondered how he would react to a visit by President Lincoln.

At the time, my wife Nina and I were writing the screenplay of *Saving Lincoln*. Nina has been a Lincoln fan since age 8, when she discovered *The Abraham Lincoln Joke Book* on her parents' shelf. And I, as a tall, red-headed immigrant, always identified with Lincoln the gangly outsider, who succeeded without help from the establishment. The first script Nina and I wrote together was *Lincoln's Hat*, the true story of Commander-in-Chief Lincoln leading our nation through the Civil War. We told it from the perspective of his hat, which doubled as a repository for Lincoln's letters, notes and other secrets. We worked on that project for two years. It was sparking interest around town when Steven Spielberg announced he was making a Lincoln movie, based on an unpublished book by Doris Kearns Goodwin and starring Tom Hanks. *Lincoln's Hat* died.

We picked ourselves up, and made the independent film, *When Do We Eat?* Our Passover comedy became a cult hit and for many people, an annual tradition. We never lost our desire, however, to tell Lincoln's story. Years went by and Mr. Spielberg had not made his film, yet no one would help us make ours because he might move forward at any moment. It didn't matter that Mr. Spielberg himself said, "The subject of Lincoln is inexhaustible." So long as his movie was possible, ours remained impossible.

We finally opted to move forward on our own. As independent filmmakers, we would find an independent way to make a Lincoln film. Having grown as writers, we revisited *Lincoln's Hat* and realized we could do better. A hat is not an emotional point of view. We reopened our Lincoln books, and became fascinated by Ward Hill Lamon, a Southerner large in both size and personality. Lamon was Lincoln's "particular friend" in Illinois and his closest companion during the White House years. The Secret Service did not yet exist, and after the first assassination attempt in 1861, Lamon appointed himself the President's bodyguard.

Lamon saved Lincoln repeatedly from murder and kidnap plots, while soothing the President's tormented soul with his banjo and good cheer. Lamon was not present at Ford's Theatre that fateful night in April 1865 because Lincoln had sent him on a mission to Richmond, but it is Lamon who ultimately redefines that tragic event in a surprising and uplifting way.

From Lamon's perspective we embarked on a new script, *Saving Lincoln*. As we worked, there was one question in the back of my mind at all times, "How will I tell this epic tale on an indie budget?" I spent hundreds of hours studying photographs in the online division of the Library of Congress in order to understand the world Lincoln and Lamon occupied. One night I zoomed deep into that hospital image, and settled my cursor beside the emaciated boy at the back of the ward. I doubt anyone had thought about him in over a century. And then it hit me.

Just as I was moving my cursor through a 150 year old image, so I could move my camera. Why recreate the Civil War world when it's already been photographed by pioneers like Mathew Brady and Alexander Gardner? I would use their photos as my sets. I am thankful that my visionary producers, Horatio Kemeny and Reuben Lim, sparked to this visual idea, as well as the emotional approach of our script.

We began testing and pre-visualization, creating mock-ups of this new kind of film. One of the tests caught my eye: a close-up of a hand penning a letter. The hand was in color, the background in black & white. I loved this hybrid look because it captured the bigger-than-life tone of Lamon's memoir, *Recollections of Abraham Lincoln*.

The hybrid approach also allowed us to "show our seams." At our budget, we couldn't maintain *Avatar*-style visual effects for every shot in the movie. This new approach would make it clear that we were going for something different; blending theater and film into a stylized reality. The resulting look invites the audience to complete the picture with us. I named this new visual style CineCollage.

As we approached the start of production, Mr. Spielberg announced that he was finally moving forward on his Lincoln project, with major stars in every role. We knew he'd be telling a similar story, but we figured he wouldn't be doing it from Lamon's point of view, and certainly not in CineCollage. We pressed on.

I cast only actors with extensive theater experience. During production, I showed them the photographs they would eventually occupy, but they had to rely on each other to stay grounded while performing in the midst of a 140-foot green screen stage. Our cinematographer matched angles with his 19th century counterparts. We worked in a warehouse in downtown L.A. in August. Hundreds of our friends came down and put on heavy wool costumes to help us fill out the crowd scenes. We were a band of brothers and sisters sweltering in the heat, adding our faces to those of our photographic "extras," like that emaciated boy in the hospital ward. *Saving Lincoln* had truly become a film of the people.

During post-production, we collaborated with digital artists in L.A., New Orleans, Detroit, Europe and India, as well as students from the Academy of Art in San Francisco. Despite our micro-budget, hundreds of people worked on the film because the project inspired them. Toward the end, we ran a Kickstarter campaign to expand our marketing and distribution efforts. Backers stepped forward, more than 90% of them strangers who'd heard about the project online. They helped us double our Kickstarter funding goal. *Saving Lincoln* had become a film by the people.

Meanwhile, we ran a determined effort to make *Saving Lincoln* a film for the people. We launched a Facebook page and started posting content about Lincoln, the Civil War, veterans, and historical photographs every day. We reached 50,000 followers a month before the film came out. Meanwhile on our Twitter account, Ward Hill Lamon was telling stories about his own colorful life.

As we approached the end of post-production, Mr. Spielberg released *Lincoln*, a brilliant portrayal of the last four months of President Lincoln's life. As Lincoln fans, we relished his fine film. As filmmakers we couldn't believe our luck: *Saving Lincoln* would be the only feature film in decades to depict Commander-in-Chief Lincoln leading the nation through the entire Civil War. *Lincoln* and *Saving Lincoln* are complementary films.

On February 11, 2013, I traveled to Springfield, IL for a special screening of *Saving Lincoln* at the Abraham Lincoln Presidential Library and Museum. Nearly 300 people were in attendance – all of them Lincoln experts and enthusiasts. The screening was part of the Abraham Lincoln Association Symposium, held annually on Lincoln's birthday. The invitation has prestige: the ALA Symposium's featured speaker a few years earlier was President Obama. Everyone present was highly knowledgeable about the 16th President's life and times, and committed to protecting his legacy. I was told this was the toughest crowd I would ever face.

I sat in the back, anxiously wondering what the audience was thinking as the film unspooled. When it ended, the room erupted into an extended standing ovation. It was a moment Nina and I had worked toward for 12 years – a pinnacle moment.

When I asked people what they liked about *Saving Lincoln*, they mentioned both its accuracy and the new kind of film experience it offers. They were deeply moved by the story and performances, and seeing it all transpire in the original locations gives the film a level of authenticity they found remarkable.

Two days later, we had our Los Angeles premiere before a crowd of 600. Though many were friends and supporters, I was most gratified by the response of their guests, who didn't know what to expect. They said they were touched by the very human Lincoln presented from his closest friend's perspective, and that seeing it all unfold within the vintage photographic world was almost like experiencing a live show.

Saving Lincoln opened in limited release on Presidents Day Weekend, 2013, and the reviews came in. Michael Medved called the film "Ingenious, original, and impressive," and when he interviewed me on his radio show, he said *Saving Lincoln* "is an important film that must be seen." Jeffrey Lyons said, "Visually innovative and superbly acted." Kirk Honeycutt said, "Provocative and arresting." Neil Genzlinger of the New York Times praised Tom Amandes (who plays Lincoln) for his low-key approach to the Gettysburg Address, which "elevates the words." And the illustrious Harold Holzer, author/editor of 44 books on Lincoln and the Civil War, called it "brilliant and entirely factual... a brave, tough, and incisive film."

Perplexingly, some young critics derided the film's stylized look. They misunderstood the film's visual language, and accused it of looking slapdash. A writer for the Village Voice actually gave us a 0 out of 100. He completely missed the emotional experience others were having in theaters. Reading his vicious remarks about my work was painful, but I took solace in similar reactions received by pioneers like e.e. cummings, Henri Matisse, and Igor Stravinsky. My favorite quote comes from Raymond Chandler who said, "The average critic never recognizes an achievement when it happens. He explains it after it has become respectable."

Nevertheless, it's the audience that always matters most. People came to see the film in theaters two and three days in a row. They sat through all the credits just to extend the experience a little more. And we are still receiving thank you notes from people who tell us *Saving Lincoln* moved them to tears.

For Nina and me, a mom & pop filmmaking shop, it's all a bit overwhelming and profoundly gratifying. We owe a debt to Abraham Lincoln, Ward Hill Lamon and all the soldiers who fought and died for the freedoms we now enjoy. We are also profoundly grateful to everyone who joined us in creating *Saving Lincoln* - a uniquely American film, made of the people, by the people and for the people.

Acknowledgments

We wish to thank the many exceptional people who made *Saving Lincoln* possible, especially Horatio & Jackie Kemeny for their patronage, vision, and support.

Profound thanks also...

To Reuben Lim for his creativity, courage, and humanity in guiding our ship safely to port;

To Tom Amandes, for sinking himself so deeply into the role of Abraham Lincoln, from walking the streets of Springfield at night to learning the President's penmanship;

To Lea Coco, for personifying the audacious, aristocratic, faithful and musical Ward Hill Lamon;

To Penelope Ann Miller, for reviving the romantic, sweet and vivacious side of Mary Todd Lincoln that was all but forgotten in American culture;

To Creed Bratton, Saidah Arrika Ekulona, Bruce Davison, Robert Craighead, Josh Stamberg, Lew Temple, Jonathan Roumie, Ally Anderson, Steven Brand, Michael Maize, Adam Croasdell, Marcus Freed, Joshua Rush, Elijah Nelson and every other member of our supremely talented, historically attuned and hard-working cast;

To Brooks D. Simpson, for his wise, insightful and nuanced answers to our questions, no matter how many we asked, and for believing in *Saving Lincoln* when it counted most;

To Kristian Hansen, for presiding over the VFX depot with devotion and panache,

To Daniel Land, for creating so many shots that define CineCollage and the unique look of *Saving Lincoln* – we salute you, suh!

To Catherine Tate, Ryan Bauer and their team at the Academy of Art University for creating and perfecting so many beautiful shots;

To Mark Adler, for reconvening with your pencil and writing tunes that will live forever;

To Willie Aron, for creating jam sessions on the set and in the studio that tug at our heart strings;

To Dave Alvin, whose haunting *Battle Hymn* transcends time and location;

To Alex Naufel, Mathew Brady and Alexander Gardner for painting the story of Lincoln and Lamon with living light;

To Carin Jacobs for dressing the Lincolneers so beautifully, and to Gabor Norman for surrounding them in an equally beautiful and tactile world;

To Yada Khoongumjorn and Ali Naqvi for lending their creativity and dedication to this book;

To Harold Holzer for educating, enlightening and entertaining us with his trove of knowledge and wit;

To Larry Weatherford, an expert on both Lincoln and Lamon, who went above and beyond to share his vast knowledge with us and our cast;

To all our other historical consultants, who gave generously of their time to help us ensure authenticity:

Timothy App
Michael Burlingame
Barry Cauchon
Rodney O. Davis
Brian Dirck
Eric Foner
Mannie Gentile
Allen Guelzo
John Heiser
James McPherson
Ann Mueller
Rea Andrew Redd
Harry Smeltzer
Chris Wehner
Samuel Wheeler
Eric J. Wittenberg
Bob Zeller

To Carl Sandburg, for capturing so much more than the facts;

To Bob Willard for sharing his invaluable insight, and our love of Abraham Lincoln;

To the Lamon/Gold family for their support;

To the Library of Congress, Helena Zinkham, and everyone else who works at that magnificent institution for keeping our history alive;

To Carla Knorowski and the Abraham Lincoln Presidential Library & Museum for bringing Mr. Lincoln back to the people;

To Matt Stasior, who was there from the beginning - a true and trusted friend;

To the Meserve-Kunhardt family for their work in preserving our national heritage;

To Operation Gratitude for partnering with us to bring *Saving Lincoln* to our troops;

To Marcus Freed for Lamonizing our ceremonies – a brilliant emcee, a ready wit, and a good friend;

To Olga Tsapina for granting us access to Lamon's papers at the Huntington Library;

To our parents, our children and all the members of our family who've been supportive and encouraging for so many years;

To our Kickstarter backers who believed in *Saving Lincoln* before they saw it, and stepped up to help us bring this unique film into the world;

To our Facebook fans who have formed a vibrant community around our shared passion for Abraham Lincoln, our troops, Civil War history and pioneering photography;

To Ward Hill Lamon for saving Lincoln from threats both physical and emotional;

To Abraham Lincoln for his courageous service to our nation;

And most of all, we thank God, without Whom nothing is possible.

Note from the Library of Congress

Digitizing Civil War Photographs at America's Library
by
Helena Zinkham

In my job as Chief of the Prints & Photographs Division at the Library of Congress in Washington, D.C., I have the privilege of working with 15 million pictures, including more than 25,000 pictures from the American Civil War. The creators of the movie *Saving Lincoln* relied on many of our images to tell their story. The result is an exceptional example of how historical photos can not only illustrate the past but become an integral part of the visual presentation.

The Library of Congress is America's national library. We welcome visitors who are able to come to Washington, DC, and work with our collections in person. We have also digitized as much Civil War material as we can. No matter where you are, you have access to copies of the photos, eye-witness drawings, engravings, and lithographs at any time of day. The Web address for the Prints & Photographs collections is www.loc.gov/pictures. Many other kinds of Civil War materials are available too, including the papers of Abraham Lincoln, slave narratives, band music, and maps.

One of the best historical sources for *Saving Lincoln* is also one of the great treasures at the Library of Congress - the unique camera negatives created by such master photographers as Alexander Gardner, George Barnard, Timothy O'Sullivan, and Mathew Brady's staff. When high resolution digital cameras became affordable, we acted quickly to have more than 6,000 negatives copied. In 2002, John Stokes and the photographic experts at his JJT firm developed a special overhead camera capture system to ensure exceptional quality in the scans.

Since scanning the glass negatives, the Library has also digitized thousands of photographic prints, drawings, and lithographs to round out the story of the Civil War. But the glass negatives remain a favorite resource because they provide such great image clarity. The head of our reference section had tears in her eyes the first time we opened the rich TIFF files. For years, she had used the printed Civil War photographs to answer questions from the public. Now she could see far more than even a magnifying glass revealed from a print, including the individual facial expressions of wounded soldiers after the battle of Fredericksburg.

Figure 1. Wagons and camera of Sam A. Cooley, U.S. photographer, Department of the South. Glass negative by unidentified photographer, 1861-1865. Library of Congress, Prints & Photographs Division

It was an exciting feeling to realize that we were opening up a new world. Our Civil War photographs have long appeared in many books and movies. They're not a secret or hidden collection. But digitizing the original negatives revealed more information than had been visible before. Among the one million pictures digitized from all parts of our collections, the Civil War negatives are a perennial favorite.

Figure 2. Close-up view of negative taken at Antietam by Alexander Gardner, 1862. Photograph by Phil Michel, 2013. Library of Congress, Prints & Photographs Division.

During the Civil War, photographers made their own negatives using a process developed in the 1850s. This type of negative is often called a wet plate, because the image had to be exposed before the emulsion dried. The primary physical characteristic is a sheet of glass, typically 8 x 10 inches or smaller and one-eighth inch thick. One side of the transparent plate is hand-coated with a light-sensitive emulsion consisting of a collodion mixture and a silver nitrate solution. The surface has a milky brownish tone.

Figure 3. Original glass plate negative for President Lincoln on Battlefield of Antietam, October, 1862. Photograph by Phil Michel, 2013. Library of Congress, Prints & Photographs Division.

As with any negative, the polarity is reversed from what our eyes see—what is dark in the real world appears light in the negative. To make the online display useful, we flip the polarity and present the negative as a "positive." It's as if the digital file is a print from the negative. One thing we don't do—we don't edit the images. You will notice scratches, cracks, emulsion tears, and missing corners caused by many years of use before the negatives came to the Library in 1943. We present the entire, uncropped negative in a neutral way, with a goal of legible content. That way each user has the opportunity to start from an authentic representation of the original photograph and then edit to suit the purposes of a particular publication or product.

Figure 4. President Lincoln on Battlefield of Antietam, October, 1862. Albumen print by Alexander Gardner. In Gardner's Photographic Sketch Book of the War. Library of Congress, Prints & Photographs Division

In the movie *Saving Lincoln* the images captured so long ago on sheets of glass have become life-size characters in the story. A new way of experiencing the power of historical photographs has been created that also shows the importance of what a library, archive, or museum can contribute to society. At the Library of Congress, we work hard to preserve the "real thing"—the authentic artifact. We also provide universal access through digital images, so that new creative works can inspire fresh connections between the past and the present and also deepen our understanding of how history happened.

Please come visit the Library of Congress collections online or in person! If you've already been to America's library, it's always worth a second look. We acquire more Civil War photographs each year, and the online collections continue to grow.

SAVING LINCOLN

A Screenplay

by

Nina Davidovich & Salvador Litvak

"The better part of one's life consists of his friendships."
- Abraham Lincoln

Fort Stevens was one of a ring of forts surrounding Washington. On July 12, 1864 the capital city was attacked by Confederate cavalry, and President Lincoln was urged to flee to safety. Instead, he ascended the parapet at Fort Stevens and stood directly in the line of fire, even as other men fell around him. We felt that if we could understand Lincoln's thinking at that moment, we might unlock the secret to this extraordinary and enigmatic man.

Fort Stevens north of Washington, D.C., glass plate negative, 1864, National Archives.

EXT. FORT STEVENS - DAY

Clouds of black smoke. Cannon FIRE. A Union fort is under attack.

>   WARD HILL LAMON (V.O.)
>   The bloody War of the Rebellion was
>   in its fourth long year when the
>   enemy launched an attack upon
>   Washington City itself.

On the parapet, ARTILLERY MEN fire at the approaching CONFEDERATES.

SUPER: WASHINGTON, DC - 1864

PRESIDENT ABRAHAM LINCOLN, 55, gaunt and haunted, strides toward the fort.

Just behind him comes U.S. MARSHAL WARD HILL LAMON, 36, dashing, herculean, and agitated as hell.

>   WARD HILL LAMON
>   (Southern accent)
>   No President has ever stood on the
>   field of battle!

Lincoln keeps moving through the chaos.

>   WARD HILL LAMON (CONT'D)
>   Your place, suh, is on that boat!

Lincoln enters the fort and heads for the parapet.

Lamon jumps in front of the President, arresting his progress, and glares into Lincoln's grey eyes:

>   WARD HILL LAMON (CONT'D)
>   Must Mary bury another Lincoln?!

>   LINCOLN
>   (to nearby OFFICER)
>   Lieutenant, remove Marshal Lamon
>   from the fort!

TWO SOLDIERS grab Lamon and pull him away.

>   WARD HILL LAMON
>   Lincoln! LINCOLN!

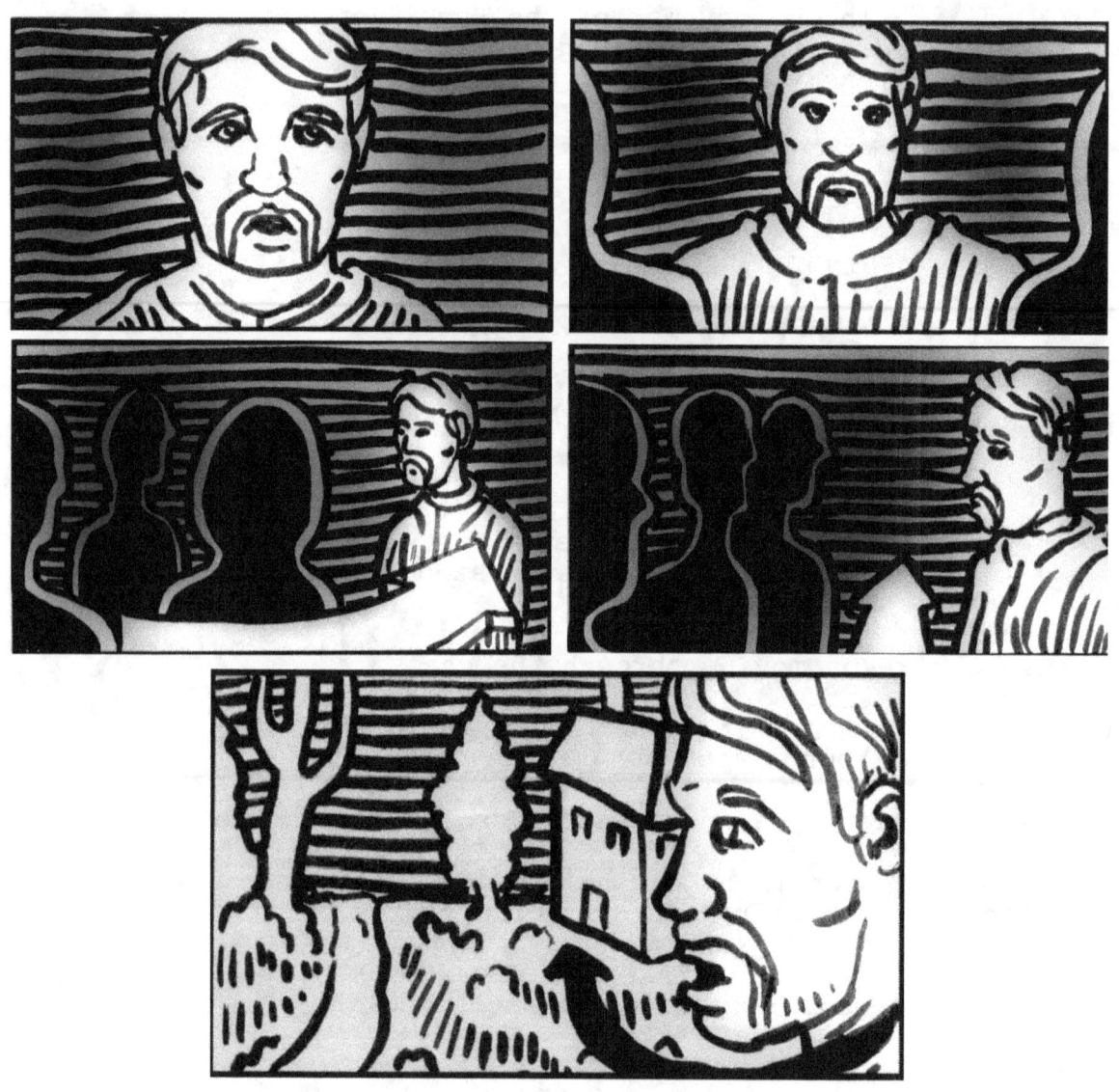

Scene 2 - INT. STATEHOUSE - NIGHT
Camera starts in close on Lamon, pulls out and dollys past the shadowy profiles of his accusers, then swoops back in towards Lamon. As we come close and begin the flashback to the rural road, the background behind Lamon changes from the dark, cavernous statehouse to a country road at dusk.

Struggling mightily, Lamon manages to throw off one soldier.

Lincoln gets closer to the parapet.

Lamon throws off the other soldier, but an OFFICER puts a gun to his head.

> OFFICER
> (to Soldiers)
> You! You! Seize him!

They drag Lamon off.

LAMON'S POV: Lincoln mounts the steps toward the cannons' ROAR. Behind him, an Artillery Man gets hit - blood everywhere. Lincoln reaches the top. He stands directly in the line of fire.

2   INT. ILLINOIS STATEHOUSE - NIGHT - **FLASH FORWARD**   2

Gas light flickers in the middle of the night. Lamon stands in the dimly lit Great Room of the Illinois Statehouse.

He faces three SHADOW MEN, seen only from behind.

> WARD HILL LAMON
> Lord knows I valued Mr. Lincoln's
> life more than my own. But keeping
> him alive these past four years...
> was nigh on impossible.

> SHADOW MAN #1
> If you so valued his life, why were
> you not at Ford's Theater?!

> WARD HILL LAMON
> To understand that, you'd have to
> hear the whole tale.

> SHADOW MAN #1
> He has no answer! He merely
> bargains for time.

> SHADOW MAN #2
> Let him speak.

Shadow Man #1 snorts in disgust, but the others wait.

Lamon takes a deep breath.

We digitally removed the statues from Statuary Hall in the U.S. Capitol to create a facsimile of the Statehouse in Springfield, IL circa 1865.

Statuary Hall, Interior, U.S. Capitol, glass plate negative, Library of Congress.

                    WARD HILL LAMON
          Oft have I wondered how I, a son of
          the South, came to be entrusted
          with that precious life when so
          many of my brethren sought to take
          it...

3   EXT. RURAL ROAD - DAY   3

A younger Lamon walks along a country road.

                    WARD HILL LAMON (V.O.)
          Was it merely an oddity of history?

Lamon wears a velvet swallowtail coat, and carries a valise
in one hand and a banjo case in the other. As the sun sets,
he approaches a country tavern blazing with light and
LAUGHTER.

                    WARD HILL LAMON (V.O.)
          *Or was the unseen hand of the
          Almighty already at work when I
          traded my native Virginia for what
          was then the wild, untamed West?*

SUPER: VERMILLION COUNTY, IL - 1847

4   INT. COUNTRY TAVERN - NIGHT   4

Lamon enters to find a crowd of rustic, laughing ILLINOISANS
gathered round a cluster of four equally bemused CIRCUIT
LAWYERS. All eyes look up at a younger, beardless Lincoln -
he is far taller than the average man, and proud of it.

                    LINCOLN
          My friends, I think I'd best retire
          before my meager pantry of stories
          is exhausted...

                    ILLINOISIANS
          Meager!...That's good!...Come
          Lincoln, another!...Tell one!

Lamon reaches the bar and stands there, watching Lincoln.

                    LINCOLN
          Your enthusiasm embarrasses me...
          And-

                    ILLINOISIANS
          There he goes!

"Was the unseen hand of the Almighty already at work when I traded my native Virginia for what was then the wild, untamed West?"
- Ward Hill Lamon, from *Saving Lincoln*
(Frame from the film)

                    LINCOLN
          And reminds me of old Bap McNabb.
          Stoic as stone he was. Never did
          moan that his crop was too short or
          his cow too lean...

Lamon reaches the bar, takes out his wallet, and pours out
its contents: three cents. He receives a very short glass of
whiskey and drinks it gratefully.

                    LINCOLN (CONT'D)
          So imagine my surprise; the richest
          man in town dies, and I found old
          Bap McNabb sobbing a river at the
          funeral. Hahaha...

Anticipating his own punch-line, Lincoln starts laughing: a
high-pitched, <u>irresistible chortle</u> that gets his audience
laughing with him long before the joke ends.

                    LINCOLN (CONT'D)
                 (imitating all the voices)
          "Bap," sez I, "was you a close
          relation of the deceased?" "No,"
          sez Bap, gulping down a sob, "No,
          no relation 't all." "Well then,
          why do you weep?" He sez, "Well,
          that's why!" HAHAHA!

Lincoln guffaws as if it's the best joke he's ever heard, and
all join him, including Lamon.

                    WARD HILL LAMON
          HAHAHA! Tremendous, suh! Tremendous!

                    LINCOLN
          'evening, stranger. Passing
          through, are you?

                    WARD HILL LAMON
          No, suh. I'm Ward Hill Lamon, J.J.
          Brown's cousin. I've come to try my
          hand as a lawyer, here in the 8th
          Circuit.

The Circuit Lawyers all lean in to inspect him, especially NED
BAKER, 36, composed and regal, and BILLY HERNDON, 29, dour,
slightly drunk, and clutching his cane.

                    LINCOLN
          Well, I should know at once you're
          a Virginian.

Cumberland Landing, Va. Group of "contrabands" (former slaves).
Glass plate negative, wet collodion. 1862. Library of Congress.

Ward Hill Lamon grew up with slaves, and his
father gave him a slave named Bob as a gift when
he graduated from college. When Lamon left
Virginia to seek his fortune as a lawyer in Illinois,
he brought Bob with him, and set him free as
soon as they crossed the state line.

CHUCKLES from the crowd, especially the youngest of the
Circuit Lawyers, LEONARD SWETT, 20's.

                    BILLY HERNDON
          Was it the velvet coat?

                    LEONARD SWETT
          The white neck-cloth, I'd say.

                    LINCOLN
          Boys, you miss the matter entirely.

                    BILLY HERNDON
          Must be the soft hands.

                    LINCOLN
          Now, while it may be certain our
          young limb of the law here has
          never split a rail-

                    WARD HILL LAMON
          Beg pardon, suh, but I have done a
          deal of manual labor in my time.

                    BILLY HERNDON
          Oh? Was it thirsty work
          superintending your slaves?

LAUGHS throughout the tavern.

                    WARD HILL LAMON
          No, suh! I detest slave labor!

                    NED BAKER
          My, my, a nerve has been touched.

                    LINCOLN
          I believe you're right, Ned.
          Counselor Lamon, I apologize for
          any offense we may have given.

                    WARD HILL LAMON
          Very kind, suh. I accept.

                    LINCOLN
          And I beg that you will indulge
          these gentlemen of the bar, and our
          fellow Illinoisians, by showing us
          a bit of your claw-hammer.

                    WARD HILL LAMON
          My claw-hammer, suh?

From childhood, Lincoln loved to make people laugh. He remembered every joke he heard, and as a young man loitered at the local general store to hone his technique on the customers. Some of his material came from "Joe Miller's Jest Book", a wildly popular collection of witticisms, first published in England in the 18th century.

The term "claw-hammer" has two meanings: a swallowtail coat, and a heavy-handed style of banjo-picking.

                    LINCOLN
          Indeed.

More than a bit puzzled, Lamon shrugs. He turns, and presents
his backside to show off his velvet, swallowtail coat.

                    WARD HILL LAMON
          English of course. Not entirely *au
          courant*, but I hope the fit flatters.

Lincoln does a double take, then breaks into that wonderful,
infectious LAUGHTER. All soon join in, though no one is sure
why they are laughing. Lamon clearly wonders whether he ought
to take offense.

                    LINCOLN
               (struggling for composure)
          The fit flatters! Hahaha...Oh, that
          is good! Counselor Lamon, if you
          please, a <u>Virginia</u> claw-hammer. West-
          ern Virginia, if I do not mistake?

                    WARD HILL LAMON
          Ohhhhhhhhhhhhhh.....hahahahahaha....

Now all are mystified indeed as some mutual understanding
connects Lamon and Lincoln.

                    WARD HILL LAMON (CONT'D)
               (to Ned Baker)
          Your chair, suh, if I may?

The puzzled Baker gets up. Lamon sets the chair before him.
Places his banjo case on it. Removes the well used instrument.

                    WARD HILL LAMON (CONT'D)
          I'm more of an up and down picker
          myself, but if it's a West Virginia
          claw-hammer you wish to hear...

Lamon's right hand assumes a <u>claw-like shape</u> to support the
picking finger, and then assaults his banjo with gusto.

His MUSIC fills the room, and gets every toe 'a tapping. But
then just as suddenly, he stops.

                    WARD HILL LAMON (CONT'D)
          I find myself in need of
          lubrication.

                    NED BAKER
               (handing him a drink)
          With the blessing, counselor.

Scene 5 Storyboard- EXT. ALLEY - DAY
Lincoln and Baker play handball against
a wall. CRANE up to Lincoln's office.

                    WARD HILL LAMON
          Handsome of you, suh. I thank you.

He quaffs it, and with a rich, *a capella* voice begins:

                    WARD HILL LAMON (CONT'D)
               (sings)
          When I was young, I used to wait

                    LINCOLN
               (joining in)
          On my master and hand him his plate

                    LAMON & LINCOLN
               (singing together)
          Pass him the jug when he got dry
          And brush away the blue-tail fly.

Then with a full-force claw-hammer, Lamon leads them all:

                    ALL
          Jimmy crack corn, and I don't care,
          Jimmy crack corn, and I don't care,
          Jimmy crack corn, and I don't care,
          My master's gone away!

While the song continues, Lincoln dances an ungainly jig with
a far more graceful Ned Baker. They try to get Billy Herndon
hopping too, but the belligerent Herndon sticks to his drink.

                    WARD HILL LAMON (V.O.)
          Mr. Lincoln was always a great
          favorite in this region, but the
          man he admired most was Ned Baker.

5   EXT. ALLEY - DAY   5

Lincoln and Baker, sleeves rolled up, enjoy a fast-paced game
of handball.

                    WARD HILL LAMON (V.O.)
          One sprung from a dirt-farm, the
          other from the British upper class.
          Yet they shared sport, law, and
          politics. Ned became such a close
          friend of the Lincolns, they named
          their son, Edward Baker Lincoln, in
          his honor.

Lincoln misses a tough shot, and claps Baker on the back.

Lincoln was notorious among fellow lawyers for undercharging his clients, thereby decreasing the monetary value of their own labor and bringing down profits for everyone.

Scene 8 Storyboard - EXT. COURTHOUSE - DAY
Lincoln receives thanks from Client and departs. PULL BACK as
Client turns to find Lamon, who is there to demand overdue fees.

INT. LINCOLN'S SPRINGFIELD OFFICE - DAY

Lincoln sits at his conference table, staring vacantly.
Herndon, working at the same table, looks over and frowns.

                    WARD HILL LAMON (V.O.)
          When that child died of
          consumption, Mr. Lincoln suffered
          from a protracted melancholy,
          alarming all of us who loved him,
          particularly Mrs. Lincoln.

7   INT. LINCOLN'S HOUSE - NIGHT   7

With the same empty expression, Lincoln leaves his dinner
untouched. MARY LINCOLN, 30's, pretty, pert and hyper-
intelligent, looks on in concern.

                    WARD HILL LAMON (V.O.)
          Fortunately, it was at just this
          time that yours truly had arrived.

Mary answers a KNOCK at the door. Lamon enters, playing an
upbeat tune on his banjo.

                    MARY
              (Southern accent)
          Oh, Mr. Lamon, so good of you to
          come! Look, Lamon's here!

Lincoln is soon smiling.

                    WARD HILL LAMON (V.O.)
          In short, I had the same effect
          upon him that whiskey has upon me.

8   EXT. COURTHOUSE - DAY   8

A PORTLY CLIENT thanks Lincoln profusely in front of the
courthouse.

                    WARD HILL LAMON (V.O.)
          I soon became Mr. Lincoln's law
          partner, and though he was my
          senior by eighteen years, there was
          one important particular in which I
          was, to a marvelous degree, his
          acknowledged superior.

The Client turns to leave, and he finds himself face to face
with an intimidating Lamon.

In 1854, Stephen Douglas, the Democratic Senator from Illinois, introduced The Kansas-Nebraska Act, which enabled new territories to vote for or against slavery. The bill was hotly debated in Congress, and passed 113 to 100. Pro- and anti-slavery agitators poured into Kansas, hoping to influence the vote. The pro-slavery men included a faction known as "border ruffians."

Violence broke out in "Bleeding Kansas" in 1856 when John Brown and his band of radical abolitionists killed five pro-slavery settlers.

                    WARD HILL LAMON
                  (to Client)
        Time you paid your bill, suh.

12   EXT. COUNTRY TAVERN   12

        A large rustic tavern.

13   INT. COUNTRY TAVERN - DAY   13

        At a corner table, Lincoln reads a newspaper article to Lamon
        and Herndon. He has to speak up in order to be heard over the
        drunken clamor of four BORDER RUFFIANS sitting nearby.

                    LINCOLN
                  (reading a newspaper)
        "...abolitionist settlers, led by
        one John Brown-"

                    BORDER RUFFIAN RINGLEADER
        Drink up, boys! Kansas ain't
        gittin' closer if we's standin'
        here!

                    LINCOLN
                  (reading)
        "...killed five pro-slavery men in
        the incident. Each of the victims
        was hacked to death by a
        broadsword."

                    BILLY HERNDON
                  (glancing at Ruffians)
        Just desserts I say!

                    WARD HILL LAMON
        You, suh, are a shameless
        anarchist!

                    BILLY HERNDON
        To hate slavery is not anarchy - it
        is morality!

                    WARD HILL LAMON
        The practice is wrong and archaic.
        And it will die of its own accord.
        But to foment bloody revolution is
        irresponsible and pig-headed!

                    BILLY HERNDON
        Phuh! You are a stone-hearted
        cracker. John Brown is a hero!

        One of the Border Ruffians approaches their table.

                            9.

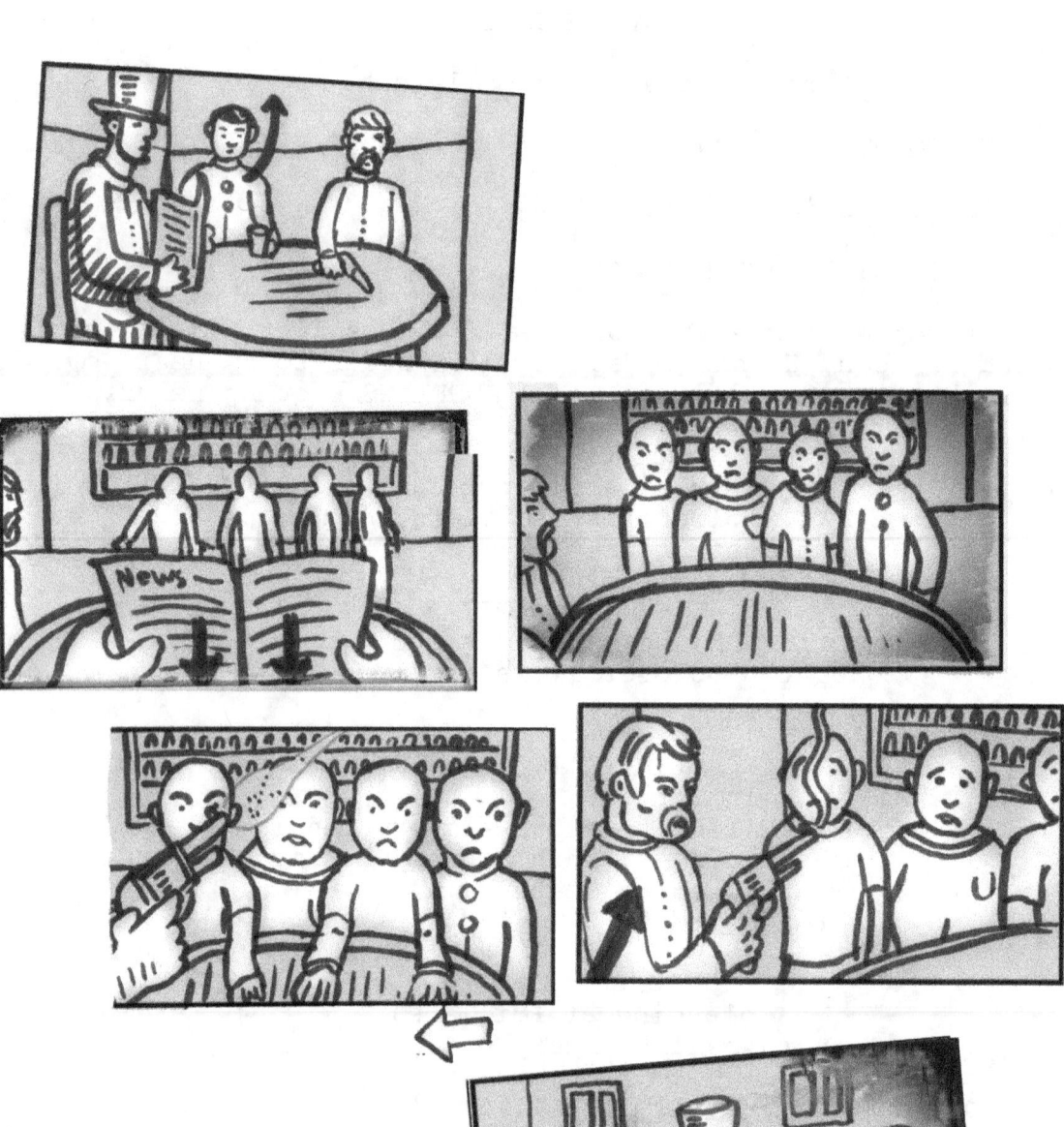

Scene 13 Storyboard - INT. COUNTRY TAVERN - DAY
Lincoln sits near the spot where he was standing in scene 4 reading the
paper. Herndon to his left, Lamon to Herndon's left. When Lincoln puts down
the paper, he sees four Ruffians at the bar and they will approach into their
CU. At climax, Lamon's gun rises into view and FIRES.

>   BORDER RUFFIAN RINGLEADER
>   When I gets to Kansas, I will shoot
>   John Brown twixt the eyes.

>   BILLY HERNDON
>   Slither on back to Kentucky, you no-
>   account ruffian.

>   BORDER RUFFIAN RINGLEADER
>   Boys, looks like we found us a
>   abolitionist.

>   BILLY HERNDON
>   And proud of it!

Herndon starts to rise but Lincoln restrains him.

>   LINCOLN
>   Gentlemen, this debate appears
>   unlikely to remain civil. Why not
>   pass on through?

Herndon pulls the handle from his cane, revealing a slender
dagger.

>   BILLY HERNDON
>   Or slither on back to Kentucky.

The ruffian pulls out a huge bowie knife.

>   BORDER RUFFIAN RINGLEADER
>   I will cut your tongue!

But Lamon produces a pistol and FIRES into the ceiling. He
points it at the Ruffian Ringleader's head.

>   WARD HILL LAMON
>   This debate, suh, is over.

The ruffians glare back, but they start to shuffle away.

Lamon puts away his gun.

>   WARD HILL LAMON (V.O.)
>   In reality, of course, the debate
>   was just getting started.

14   EXT. POLITICAL RALLY - DAY   14

Lincoln shares the speakers' platform with STEPHEN DOUGLAS,
40's, short in stature, gigantic in stage presence.

Abraham Lincoln, October 1, 1858
Photographic print, gelatin silver
Library of Congress.

The Lincoln-Douglas debates of 1858 were a series of seven debates between Abraham Lincoln, Republican candidate for Senator in Illinois, and incumbent Democratic Senator Stephen Douglas. Lincoln lost that election, but the ensuing popularity of the published debates led to Lincoln's nomination for President in 1860.

In the AUDIENCE, people hold various signs supporting Lincoln
or Douglas for Senate. Lamon, Herndon and JUDGE DAVID DAVIS,
40's, imposing, sit among the VIP's behind the debaters.

SUPER: OTTAWA, IL - AUG 21, 1858

                                                        MONTAGE:

                    STEPHEN DOUGLAS
               (to crowd)
          Would you turn our beautiful State
          into a free Negro colony?

                    DOUGLAS SUPPORTERS
          NO!

                    LINCOLN
          Let us discuss Kansas. It is <u>wrong</u>
          to introduce slavery there!

                    LINCOLN SUPPORTERS
          HEAR HEAR!

                    STEPHEN DOUGLAS
          Do you wish your daughters to marry
          free Negro men?

                    DOUGLAS SUPPORTERS
          NEVER!

                    LINCOLN
          I hate the monstrous injustice of
          slavery. And I hate how it enables
          the enemies of free institutions,
          with plausibility, to taunt us
          Americans as hypocrites!

HUGE APPLAUSE from his supporters. Lamon nods proudly.

                    STEPHEN DOUGLAS
          Then, by God, do not vote for my
          opponent, because it was he who
          abolitionized the Old Whig Party,
          and he who created this new, Black
          Republican Party, and he who will
          declare the Negro your equal!

                    DOUGLAS SUPPORTERS
          DOUGLAS FOREVER! LINCOLN NEVER!

Lincoln changes gears, and draws them in...

                              11.

The script originally called for a montage of election signs and posters, but our final choice was to show a newspaper with a headline proclaiming Lincoln president.

Hon. Abraham Lincoln, 1860
Wood engraving, Library of Congress.

                              LINCOLN
                    The economic reality of slavery
                    does not admit to forced or rapid
                    abolition, and I do not advocate
                    for any such radical course. But I
                    will not stand by and have it
                    expand into any new territory!

Lincoln's supporters erupt in RAUCOUS CHEERING.

                              WARD HILL LAMON (V.O.)
                    Leave slavery alone where it is but
                    forbid it from spreading. A common-
                    sense position that made national
                    headlines. He lost his Senate race
                    with Douglas, but just two years
                    later the American people bestowed
                    upon him the highest office ever
                    given to a man of such humble
                    origin.

MONTAGE of campaign posters and headlines: LINCOLN FOR
PRESIDENT; LINCOLN ELECTED; LET THE PEOPLE REJOICE.

15   INT. LINCOLN'S SPRINGFIELD OFFICE - NIGHT   15

Campaign banners and buttons reading "Lincoln for President"
are scattered about the room. Lamon helps Lincoln pack.

                              WARD HILL LAMON
                    Lincoln, I have been thinking how I
                    may best serve our country.

                              LINCOLN
                    Have you now?

                              WARD HILL LAMON
                    I believe Ben Franklin's old job
                    would suit.

                              LINCOLN
                         (laughing)
                    Ambassador to France!

                              WARD HILL LAMON
                    Ambassador to France. I only wish
                    my wife had lived to see the day.

Lincoln pauses his work.

                              LINCOLN
                    God rest Angeline's soul, Hill.
                    Mary and I miss her terribly.
                         (MORE)

Angeline Turner was Ward Hill Lamon's first wife. She died in 1859, leaving an infant daughter, Dorothy. Dorothy Lamon was raised by her aunt in Danville, IL. Dorothy later compiled her father's personal writings about Lincoln into *Recollections of Abraham Lincoln*, one of the principal sources for this screenplay.

Elmer Ephraim Ellsworth (1837-1861) led a nationally renowned drill team whose red uniforms were patterned after those of the French Zouaves.

Elmer Ephraim Ellsworth, 1861
Wood engraving, Library of Congress.

> LINCOLN (CONT'D)
> But as for Ambassador, the fact is,
> I want you to come to Washington
> with me.

Now Lamon pauses.

> WARD HILL LAMON
> In what capacity?

> LINCOLN
> I don't know yet, but a fight may
> be coming and if it does, it will
> be handy to have you around.

> WARD HILL LAMON
> Hmph. ...Second administration?

> LINCOLN
> (laughing)
> My friend, if there is a second
> administration, and you and I both
> live to see it, then yes, you shall
> make a superb Ambassador to France!

16   EXT. GREAT WESTERN RAILWAY STATION - DAY   16

A grey day and a quiet CROWD. A special train is draped with
soggy red, white and blue ribbons.

> WARD HILL LAMON (V.O.)
> *The fight came quickly. Seven*
> *states left the Union, and seven*
> *more embarked upon the same course.*

Lincoln's entourage, including Judge Davis and COL. ELMER
ELLSWORTH, 24, handsome and spry, emerge on a platform behind
the train's caboose.

> WARD HILL LAMON (V.O.)
> *Sacks of letters arrived daily,*
> *cursing Mr. Lincoln for destroying*
> *our nation and promising to destroy*
> *him in return.*

Mary Lincoln and her sons, WILLIE, 11, sensitive, and TAD, 8,
rambunctious, take their place on the platform.

> WARD HILL LAMON (V.O.)
> *One fellow even demonstrated his*
> *intent by sending Mrs. Lincoln a*
> *painting of her husband: tarred,*
> *feathered and hanging by the neck.*

"My friends, no one, not in my situation, can appreciate my feeling of sadness at this parting. To this place, and the kindness of these people, I owe everything. Here I have lived a quarter of a century, and have passed from a young to an old man. Here my children have been born, and one is buried. I now leave, not knowing when, or whether ever, I may return, with a task before me greater than that which rested upon Washington. Without the assistance of the Divine Being who ever attended him, I cannot succeed. With that assistance I cannot fail. Trusting in Him who can go with me, and remain with you, and be everywhere for good, let us confidently hope that all will yet be well. To His care commending you, as I hope in your prayers you will commend me, I bid you an affectionate farewell."

- Abraham Lincoln, Farewell Address
Springfield, IL, February 11, 1861

Lincoln emerges and faces the crowd. Filled with emotion, he removes his hat.

All men present do the same.

> LINCOLN
> My friends, no one, not in my situa-
> tion, can appreciate my feeling of
> sadness at this parting. To this
> place and the kindness of these
> people, I owe everything...

17   INT. RAILWAY STATION - DAY - CONTINUOUS   17

Herndon, Swett and another Circuit Lawyer surround Lamon like a menacing, secret society.

> LEONARD SWETT
> Hill, we intrust the sacred life of
> Mr. Lincoln to your keeping.

> WARD HILL LAMON
> I am honored, suh.

> BILLY HERNDON
> Hill, if you fail to protect him,
> never return to Illinois, for we
> will murder you on sight.

Their eyes bore into his. Lamon draws himself up to his full height.

> WARD HILL LAMON
> I will not fail him.

18   INT. RAILROAD CAR - MOVING - DAY   18

Inside a fancy club car, Lamon reads a stack of letters.

> WARD HILL LAMON
> "...lynch you, shoot you, hang you,
> burn you..."

Lamon checks his weapons: two revolvers in shoulder holsters, two pocket derringers, and a large bowie knife.

Dapper JOHN HAY, 22, passes by to join the Lincolns and Judge Davis.

> HAY
> They have seized the federal forts.
> All but Sumter in Charleston.

Willie Lincoln was the third son of Abraham and Mary Lincoln, and in personality and intellect most resembled his father. His mother described him as "a very beautiful boy, with a most spiritual expression of face."

William Walllace Lincoln
Photographic print. Library of Congress.

                         JUDGE DAVIS
          That's it then. It's war.

                         LINCOLN
          No. Traitors have seized federal
          forts. They will be prosecuted. But
          the Southern people never chose this
          course, and I will not make war on
          them.

                         MARY
          And I tell you they have already made
          war on you, father! My own brothers
          are burning Union flags!

                         LINCOLN
               (gently)
          That is free speech, not war.

                         COL. ELMER ELLSWORTH (O.S.)
          Shoulder arms!

Further up the car, Ellsworth runs Willie and Tad through an
elaborate drill with their toy rifles.

The boys spin their toy rifles well.

                         WILLIE & TAD
          One! Two!

                         JUDGE DAVIS
          He cannot order the forts retaken
          before he is inaugurated.

                         MARY
          He can announce his intentions.

                         JUDGE DAVIS
          Any such announcement will
          precipitate war!

                         LINCOLN
          So, we are to make 70 stops in 12
          days and I must neither speak nor
          remain silent. War is imminent. And
          our great American Experiment - now
          entrusted to my care - hangs by a
          thread.

All nod. Long BEAT as the train rolls east.

Lincoln finally clears his throat.

                              15.

On February 11, 1861, Lincoln boarded a special train in his Springfield home town bound for his inaugural in Washington, accompanied by friends, family, staff aides, a doctor, a telegraph operator, and in response to recent threats of violence, a formidable, unprecedented retinue of bodyguards. These included Captain George W. Hazzard, Major David Hunter, Colonel Edwin Vose "Bull Head" Sumner, and drillmaster par excellence Elmer Ephraim Ellsworth. Lincoln not only added Lamon to this imposing military roster, but made sure his friend first received an appointment from the State of Illinois as Colonel of Artillery. It was easy to understand why Lincoln wanted "Colonel" Lamon along for the most important—and perilous— journey of his life. Lamon was not only devoted; Lincoln's private secretary, John G. Nicolay, remembered him as "a man of extraordinary size and herculean strength." As the blustery, hard-drinking Lamon remarked of his relationship with Lincoln: "I may not be mighty in Counsel, but might be useful in a fight."

> \- Harold Holzer, noted Lincoln authority
> From the foreword to *Recollections of Abraham Lincoln*
> by Ward Hill Lamon (*Saving Lincoln* reissue, 2013)

                    LINCOLN (CONT'D)
                 (singing)
          *Well Old Dan Tucker was a fine old
          man...*

A CHUCKLE escapes Lamon and he reaches for his banjo.
Everyone welcomes the diversion.

                    LINCOLN (CONT'D)
          *Washed his face in a frying pan
          Combed his hair with a wagon wheel
          Died with a toothache in his heel!*

                    ALL
          *Git out the way Old Dan Tucker, He's
          too late to get his supper.
          Supper's over and breakfast cookin'
          Old Dan Tucker stand there lookin'!*

EXT. COUNTRYSIDE - DAY

The song continues as the Presidential train rolls eastward.

                    JUDGE DAVIS
          *Old Dan Tucker he got drunk
          Fell in the fire and kicked up a
          chunk
          The red hot coal was in his shoe
          Oh my Lord how the ashes flew!*

19   EXT. SPEAKER'S PLATFORM - DAY   19

Guarded by Lamon, Lincoln addresses various CROWDS.

                    LINCOLN
          Citizens of Columbus!

                    LINCOLN (CONT'D)
          Buffalo!

                    LINCOLN (CONT'D)
          Albany!

                    LINCOLN (CONT'D)
          Trenton!

Great CHEERS.

INT. RAILROAD CAR - MOVING - DAY

Judge Davis drums on Lamon's banjo case.

                              16.

The song "Old Dan Tucker" is a classic American folk tune that was first introduced by a blackface troupe called the Virginia Minstrels in 1843. Many artists have recorded this song, including Bruce Springsteen.

Hundreds of alternate verses of "Old Dan Tucker" have been catalogued. Here is one written to commemorate emancipation:

> *Ho! the car Emancipation*
> *Rides majestic thro' our nation,*
> *Bearing on its train the story;*
> *Liberty! a nation's glory.*
> *Get out the way! Every station!*
> *Freedom's car, Emancipation!*

                    ALL
Git out the way Old Dan Tucker,
He's too late to get his supper.
Supper's over and breakfast cookin'
Old Dan Tucker stand there lookin'!

Willie and Tad sing with their idol:

              WILLIE, TAD & ELLSWORTH
Old Dan Tucker went to town,
Riding a mule and leading a hound,
Hound barked, mule jumped,
Landed Ol' Dan upon a stump!

                    ALL
Git out the way Old Dan Tucker,
He's too late to get his supper.
Supper's over and breakfast cookin'
Old Dan Tucker stand there lookin'!

Mary joins in, waving her fan playfully:

                    MARY
Here's old Dan, he comes to town;
Swings the ladies round and round.
Swings one east, swings one west,
Swings with the one he loves the
best!

Lincoln takes his wife's hand and kisses it.

                    ALL
Git out the way Old Dan Tucker,
He's too late to get his supper.
Supper's over and breakfast cookin'
Old Dan Tucker stand there lookin'!

23   EXT. TRAIN PLATFORM - NIGHT   23

Outside a tiny train station, a stop-signal is raised. A MAN
IN AN OVERCOAT waits in the shadows.

Lincoln's inaugural train approaches as the song dies down.

                    ALL
Get out the way, old Dan Tucker...

24   INT. RAILROAD CAR - MOVING - NIGHT   24

As the train comes to a stop, Lamon strums and sings <u>softly</u>.

                      17.

Allan Pinkerton is famous for creating the Pinkerton National Detective Agency, the first agency of its kind, and one that is still in business today. Pinkerton pioneered essential investigative techniques such as surveillance and the use of undercover agents.

Allan Pinkerton, Antietam, Maryland, 1862
Glass plate negative, wet collodion, Library of Congress.

                    WARD HILL LAMON
          Old Dan begun early in life
          To play the banjo and the fife
          He'd lull the children all to sleep
          And then into his bunk he'd creep

Nobody notices as the Man in the Overcoat steals into the car
and approaches Lincoln's entourage.

                    MAN IN OVERCOAT
               (Scottish accent)
          Mr. Lincoln.

The man's sudden arrival alarms Lamon. He is ALLAN PINKERTON,
40's, a bearded Scottish immigrant. Lamon grabs him.

                    LINCOLN
          Hill, it's our old friend,
          Pinkerton! How are you, sir?

Lamon releases Pinkerton.

                    PINKERTON
          Mr. Lincoln. (to Mary) Ma'am.

                    LINCOLN
          How do you come to be here?

                    MAN IN OVERCOAT/PINKERTON
          Detective job for the railroad,
          sir. Mr. Lincoln, we have come to
          know, and beyond the shadow of a
          doubt, there exists an organized
          plot to assassinate ye.

Mary GASPS.

                    LINCOLN
          Balderdash. No President was ever
          assassinated.

                    PINKERTON
          The attempt will be made tomorrow,
          at the Baltimore station. A gang of
          toughs will start a fight to draw
          off the police. Assassins will then
          approach through the crowd, and
          plunge theer knives into yeer side.

                    WARD HILL LAMON
          You have evidence?

                    PINKERTON
          Here are the names.

The conspiracy to kill President-elect Lincoln has come to be known as the Baltimore Plot. The threat posed by the plot was credible, and Lincoln felt he had no choice but to enter Washington secretly if he wanted to remain alive long enough to become President. Lincoln's undignified entrance into Washington in the middle of the night was quickly dubbed the "nocturnal sneak" by newspapers, and the episode gave cartoonists and humorists good material for the first week of Lincoln's presidency. The public outcry deeply wounded Lincoln and he vowed to never again appear weak before the public.

He hands Lincoln a document.

                    MARY
          But you know of it! Surely the
          police will stop them!

                    PINKERTON
          The Chief of Police is one of them,
          Ma'am.

                    JUDGE DAVIS
          We'll change the route.

                    PINKERTON
          Ye'll not find a safe route through
          Maryland if they know ye're coming.
               (to Lincoln)
          Sir, we propose to take ye to
          Washington this very night, and
          steal a march on yeer enemies.

                    MARY
          Steal into the capital like a thief
          in the night?!

                    PINKERTON
          Would ye prefer a funeral, Ma'am?

                    JUDGE DAVIS
          The papers will shriek.

                    ELMER ELLSWORTH
          We will surround him with a
          regiment and cut our way through.

                    WARD HILL LAMON
          With Mrs. Lincoln and the boys
          aboard?
               (to Lincoln)
          The papers will praise you for
          putting their safety first.

                    PINKERTON
          It is a mob of desperate characters
          in Baltimore, Mr. Lincoln, but they
          expect ye tomorrow. Pass through
          tonight, and destroy theer plot.

Lincoln looks at his wife.

                    LINCOLN
          I believe I must.

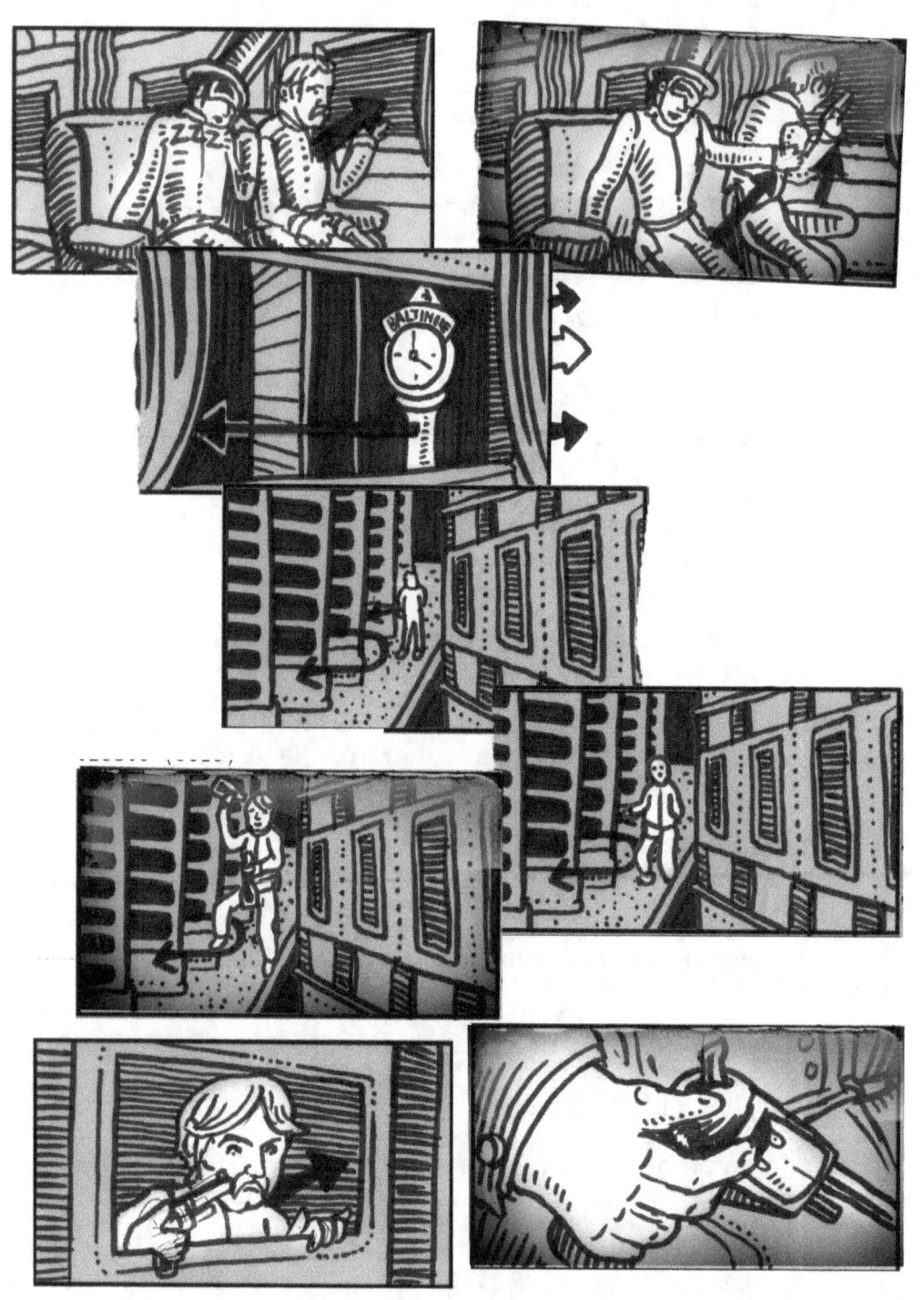

Scene 25 Storyboard - INT/EXT. BALTIMORE STATION - NIGHT
Camera skewed, music and lighting ominous, action follows script.

                    PINKERTON
        Aye. We'll change trains in
        Harrisburg. Kindly leave the hat
        behind. Ye and I will then ride on
        as private citizens.

                    WARD HILL LAMON
        I will ride with Mr. Lincoln.

                    PINKERTON
        The plan calls for one companion.

                    WARD HILL LAMON
        I have pledged my life to preserve,
        protect and defend Mr. Lincoln. I will
        ride with him.

                    PINKERTON
        Mr. President-

                    LINCOLN
        I will ride with Hill.

25   INT/EXT. BALTIMORE STATION - NIGHT   25

Lamon looks out through the window of a passenger car. Beside
him Lincoln dozes, wearing a felt cap and sleep mask.

The train pulls into a nearly deserted station at 4:00 a.m.

Lamon looks nervous as the train comes to a stop.

                    MAN'S VOICE
                (eerie, almost demented)
        In Dixie Land I'll take my stand to
        live and die in Dixie!

Lamon leans out his window to see who is singing.

LAMON'S POV: Down the platform, a SUSPICIOUS MAN disappears
behind a column.

                    SUSPICIOUS MAN (O.S.)
        Away, away, away down South in
        Dixie!

Lamon's fingers wrap around his gun.

LAMON'S POV: The Suspicious Man reappears much closer.

                    SUSPICIOUS MAN (CONT'D)
        Away, away!

To create the ominous environment of Baltimore station at night, our VFX team created a virtual puppet theatre out of a number of images collaged into a dark, atmospheric environment.

In this detail from our Scene 30 plate, the man standing next to the conductor is partially transparent, and has a ghostly trail leading off to the right. This is due to the long exposure times required for early glass plate photography. Exposure times could last over 20 seconds, and this man must have moved during that interval. In *Saving Lincoln*, we embraced these interesting textures, so a number of ghostly "photographic extras" appear throughout the film.

Lamon pulls his gun out. The Suspicious man disappears behind another column.

                    SUSPICIOUS MAN (O.S.) (CONT'D)
               Away down South in Dixie!

Lamon aims his gun, waiting for the man to come into view.

Though apparently asleep, Lincoln calmly pushes down the barrel of Lamon's gun.

                    LINCOLN
                 (murmuring)
               No doubt there will be a great time
               in Dixie by and by.

Lamon looks out the window. The man reappears up close.

                    SUSPICIOUS MAN
               I wish I was in the land of - hic!

He's a harmless drunk. Lamon is visibly relieved not to have shot him. A WHISTLE blows. The train starts moving.

30   INT. UNION TRAIN STATION - DAY   30

Early morning. The train has reached Washington D.C. COMMUTERS walk on the platform.

Lamon leads Lincoln from the train, wearing the felt cap pulled low over his eyes.

                    MAN'S VOICE (O.S.)
               You can't pull that on me.

A MAN pushes through the crowd. Lamon steps forward, fist raised, ready to attack.

                    LINCOLN
               Do not strike him! It is the new
               Senator from Oregon.

                    WARD HILL LAMON
               The new...? Ned Baker!

                    NED BAKER
               Lamon, old fellow! Welcome to
               Washington City!

Baker and Lincoln embrace warmly.

This is one of our favorite shots in the film, based on a photograph that was actually taken from the top of the finished Washington Monument around 1906. We removed all buildings over six stories to sugggest 1861, changed the angle of view, then added the balloon, monument and construction elements.

NED BAKER (CONT'D)
Now let us shove off ere we're
observed. The papers will have
their fun soon enough...

31   EXT. WASHINGTON MONUMENT - DAY   31

The Washington Monument is under construction.

WARD HILL LAMON (V.O.)
*The papers did more than have their
fun. They crucified him, saying he
was "an imbecilic, namby-pamby
coward who would make America the
laughingstock of the world for
having no better material out of
which to make a President."*

32   INT. ILLINOIS STATEHOUSE - NIGHT - **FLASH FORWARD**   32

Lamon addresses the Shadow Men.

WARD HILL LAMON
Determined to avoid any further
show of cowardice, Mr. Lincoln
flatly refused all attempts to
place guards about his person. And
it is only because I provided
companionship and musical diversion
that he tolerated my own heavily
armed presence.

We see the Shadow Men are Herndon, Swett, and Circuit Lawyer.

BILLY HERNDON
Just get on with it.

33   INT. WHITE HOUSE UPSTAIRS CORRIDOR - DAY   33

TRACKING SHOT: Camera moves past a long line of Citizens
waiting to meet the President. The line continues into the
family quarters, where Willie and Tad run by with their toy
rifles.

WARD HILL LAMON (V.O.)
*His first official act was to throw
open the doors of the Executive
Mansion to any American who desired
conversation with the President,
and seemingly all 30 millions of
them accepted the offer.*

APPROACH Lamon, now wearing the <u>badge of a U.S. Marshal</u>. He
questions an ARCHITECT about a roll of blueprints.

William H. Seward (1801-1872) was Governor of New York and a U.S. Senator before serving as Lincoln's Secretary of State. Seward was the front-runner for the Republican nomination for president in 1860, until newcomer Abraham Lincoln prevailed in a last-minute victory at the convention.

Wm. Seward, between 1861 and 1863
From an earlier engraving, photographic print on carte de visite mount. Library of Congress.

Salmon P. Chase (1808-1873) was Governor of Ohio and a U.S. Senator before serving as Lincoln's Secretary of the Treasury. He was a lawyer who first achieved prominence defending fugitive slaves. In 1864 Chase left Lincoln's cabinet to become Chief Justice of the Supreme Court.

Salmon P. Chase, between 1860 and 1865
Glass plate negative, wet collodion.
Library of Congress.

                    ARCHITECT
          They are blueprints, sir, for a
          library in Clarkstown, New York.

                    WARD HILL LAMON
          You rolled them yourself?

                    ARCHITECT
          Yes.

                    WARD HILL LAMON
          Why so tightly?

                    ARCHITECT
          So they don't unroll in the street?

Lamon grabs the plans.

34   INT. LINCOLN'S OFFICE - DAY   34

Lincoln addresses three CABINET MEMBERS seated around the
conference table.

                    LINCOLN
          Nothing will prevent war but my
          acquiescence in their secession.

A feisty Marylander, MONTGOMERY BLAIR, 40's, speaks first.

                    MONTGOMERY BLAIR
          Then it is equally plain you must
          reinforce Sumter. These cavaliers
          believe that Northern men are
          deficient in the courage necessary
          to maintain government, and they
          will be undeceived!

                    LINCOLN
          If the U.S. Army invades
          Charleston, Europe will rush in to
          defend this fledgling Confederate
          democracy from "tyranny."

Next to advise is an imposing, statesmanlike Ohioan, SALMON
P. CHASE, 50's.

                    TREASURER CHASE
          England and France love freedom,
          sir! They will never recognize a
          confederacy of slave-owners too
          indolent to farm their own land.

A subtle New Yorker with twinkling eyes, WILLIAM H. SEWARD,
60's, answers.

                            23.

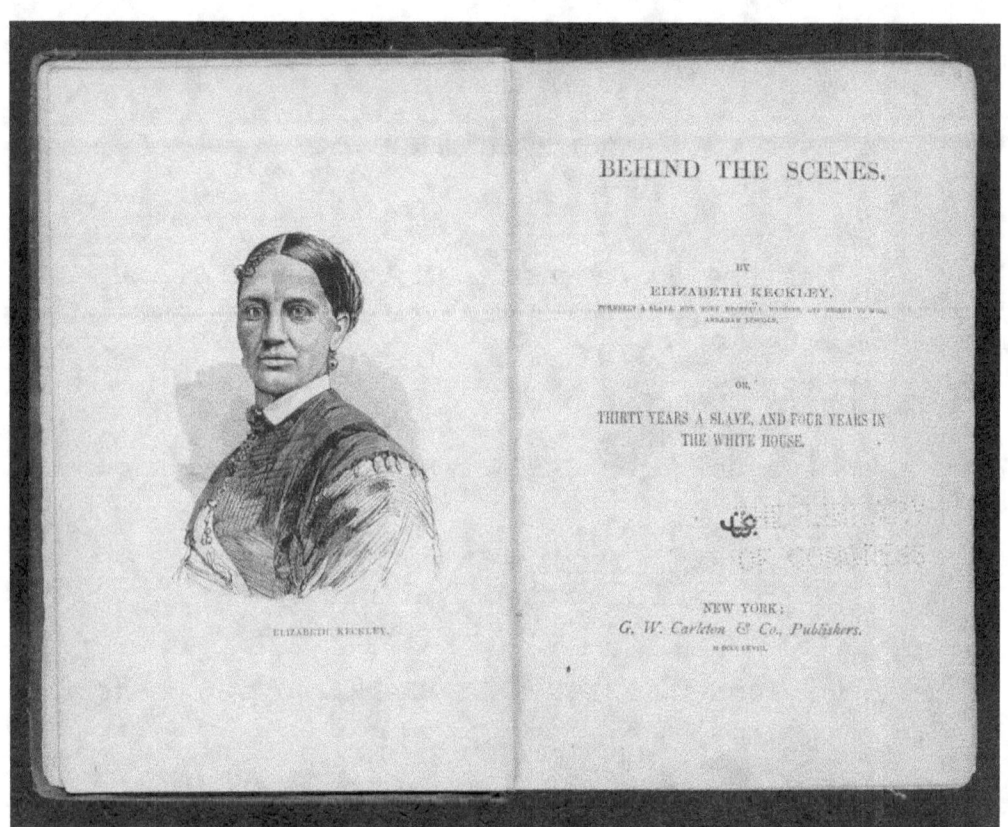

Elizabeth Keckly (her preferred spelling) was born a slave in Virginia in 1818. She became an entrepreneur who achieved great success as a dressmaker in Washington DC. Previous to working at the White House, she sewed dresses for the wives of Robert E. Lee and soon-to-be Confederate President Jefferson Davis. She was thus responsible for dressing both First Ladies of the Civil War. Image from the Library of Congress.

                    SEC. OF STATE SEWARD
          Yes, however, a stoppage of American
          cotton will reduce whole communities
          to famine, and possibly spark
          revolutions throughout Europe. Now,
          against this outcome, England and
          France will not only recognize the
          Confederate States of America, they
          will feed them, arm them, and
          reinforce them with legions of men.

                    LINCOLN
          I am Commander-in-Chief of all our
          forces. I cannot surrender a
          federal fort without a fight.

                    SEC. OF STATE SEWARD
          Then...you must invade Mexico.

All regard Seward with bewilderment.

                    LINCOLN
          Come again, Mr. Seward?

                    SEC. OF STATE SEWARD
          A foreign fight will unite North
          and South, and provide long
          distraction while we negotiate.

                    LINCOLN
          Hmph. Gentlemen, I must think.

35   INT. LINCOLN'S OFFICE - NIGHT   35

A dishevelled Lincoln paces back and forth while Lamon picks
lightly at his banjo.

                    LINCOLN
          It is a Gordian knot! Give England
          and France cause to enter the war,
          or surrender both the fort and the
          honor of my office.

                    WARD HILL LAMON
          What says your instinct?

                    LINCOLN
          My instinct says, "Find another
          choice!"

Mary suddenly bursts in, wearing a stylish dress in the
process of being altered by MRS. ELIZABETH KECKLY, 30's, a
levelheaded, African-American seamstress.

Mary Lincoln was from the illustrious Todd family of Lexington, KY. Four of her brothers fought for the Confederacy and three of them died in battle. Mary's brother-in-law, a Confederate general, was also killed in action.

Mary Todd Lincoln, 1861
Photographic print on carte de visite mount.
Library of Congress.

                    MRS. KECKLY
          Mrs. Lincoln, I fear you will be
          pricked!

Mary's gown is held together by dozens of pins, and Mrs.
Keckly holds a needle and thread still attached to one of its
seams.

                    MARY
               (holding up a newspaper)
          It is an outrage! Because my brothers
          joined the Confederacy, they charge
          me with treasonous sympathy!

                    LINCOLN
               (regarding her gown)
          Molly, you bedazzle me.

                    MARY
          I do?

                    WARD HILL LAMON
          I too am dazzled, Ma'am.

                    MARY
          Oh, it is the finest Parisian silk.

                    LINCOLN
          Excellent work, Mrs. Keckly.

                    MRS. KECKLY
          Thank-

                    MARY
          But, Father, this reporter calls me
          a confederate spy!

                    LINCOLN
          At least you're not likened to a
          simian brute as I usually-

                    MARY
          Marshal Lamon, you must arrest this
          man, shut down his paper, and clear
          my-!

Her emphatic gesture causes a dress pin to prick her.

                    MARY (CONT'D)
          OW!!!

                    MRS. KECKLY
          I'm sorry, Mrs. Lincoln, I was not
          able to secure the pins-

Abraham Lincoln was a man of simple tastes. His favorite meal was a boiled egg.

White House Kitchen, 1904
Photographic print, Library of Congress.

                    MARY
        No, Mrs. Keckly, I ought not have
        rushed off. But it is so vexing...

                    LINCOLN
        I will send this publisher a note,
        Mother, as soon as I find a way to
        stop England and France from joining
        this war.

                    MARY
        England and France are ancient,
        sovereign nations who respect a
        strong potentate. One who does more
        than "send a note!"

Lamon and Keckly look embarrassed, but Lincoln remains serene.

                    LINCOLN
        Mother, we will spare no effort to
        rectify your good name.

                    MARY
        Thank you! Good night.

She exits, pulling Mrs. Keckly by the needle and thread.

                    MRS. KECKLY
        Mr. President.

                    LINCOLN
        Mrs. Keckly.

                    LINCOLN (CONT'D)
            (to Lamon)
        It is grotesque that any would
        consider me the aggressor when
        traitors besiege my forts.

                    WARD HILL LAMON
        I am reminded of the young man
        whose aged parents had a
        considerable amount of property.

                    LINCOLN
        Oh yes. Killed the poor folks to
        get his inheritance. Judge asked
        why he should not be hanged-

                    WARD HILL LAMON
        The young man replied..."Oh please
        have mercy on me for I am a poor
        orphan!"

These men are unknown, but they remind us of Lamon and Pinkerton, who maintained an uneasy relationship throughout the Civil War. We used the background of this shot for *Scene 40*, in which a Confederate flag flies over Alexandria.

Washington, D.C. The Aqueduct bridge and Georgetown from the Virginia bank. Glass plate negative, wet collodion, between 1860 and 1865, Library of Congress.

Lincoln enjoys the joke as if he'd never heard it before.

                    LINCOLN
          HAHAHA...hmmm... Hill. That's it!
          England and France will not
          exonerate an orphan who kills his
          own parents! These Southerners are
          so hungry for war, they will fire
          first, even without provocation. So
          I will not reinforce Sumter. I will
          simply send the men food. If that
          precipitates war, I dare say, the
          ancient sovereign nations will keep
          out.

35A   INT. WHITE HOUSE KITCHEN - DAY   35A

A soft-boiled egg is delicately opened with a little knife.

                    WARD HILL LAMON (V.O.)
          *The rebels did fire first, Europe
          kept out, and Mr. Lincoln took the
          first trick.*

                    LINCOLN
          The real trick is to smash a
          little, cut a little...and dip.

Lincoln dips his toast into the open egg, and soft yolk
floods over the side.

Willie imitates his father perfectly. Tad has more trouble,
and Lamon lends a hand.

Col. Elmer Ellsworth marches in.

                    ELMER ELLSWORTH
          Mr. President, a rebel flag flies
          across the Potomac in full view of
          the Executive Mansion. It is an
          affront, sir!

                    WARD HILL LAMON
          An egregious affront.

                    ELMER ELLSWORTH
          Permission to cross the river and
          retrieve said flag, sir!

                    LINCOLN
          By all means, dear boy.

                    WILLIE
          Yippee! Let's go get it!

We used this shot for Scene 41, in which Lincoln grapples with one of the first casualties of the Civil War. The death of Elmer Ephraim Ellsworth stung the entire North, but none more than Lincoln, who counted Ellsworth as a close family friend.

Potomac River, guards at ferry landing on Mason's Island examining a pass
Glass plate negative, wet collodion, between 1860 and 1865, Library of Congress.

LINCOLN
Willie, you and Tad shall observe
this crucial mission from a
Presidential perspective.

ELMER ELLSWORTH
The flag shall be yours by noon,
sir!

LINCOLN
Godspeed.

40   EXT. WHITE HOUSE ROOF - DAY   40

Lincoln and Lamon stand on the roof of the White House with
Willie and Tad. The Lincolns peer through spyglasses, Lamon
through binoculars, all looking out across the Potomac River.

WARD HILL LAMON (V.O.)
Colonel Ellsworth always put on a
good show. His Zouave militia
thrilled the nation with their
precision drills. His friendship
gave candidate Lincoln a martial
air. And it was Ellsworth himself
who recruited the first 75,000
Union volunteers. Indeed, the war
fever had come. Even Senator Baker
joined up.

Lamon passes his binoculars to Ned Baker, now wearing the
uniform of a Union Colonel.

LINCOLN'S POV: across the Potomac, a rebel flag is lowered.

Lincoln and Willie lead long CHEERS on the roof.

Then a single, distant SHOT echoes across the water.

41   EXT. POTOMAC RIVER - DAY   41

Ellsworth's body, on a stretcher, is placed before Lincoln,
Lamon, and Baker.

LINCOLN
My boy! My boy! Was it necessary
this sacrifice should be made?

Baker hands Lincoln a blood-splattered rebel flag. Lamon puts
a hand on Lincoln's shoulder.

NED BAKER
He was carrying it down the stairs.
They shot him in the heart.

The earliest photograph of the White House, taken between 1860 and 1865.
Glass plate negative, wet collodion, Library of Congress.

LINCOLN
They will mourn that shot.

42   EXT. WHITE HOUSE - DAY   42

Fog. Lincoln stands at the foot of the White House lawn.

SUPER: JULY 22, 1861

WARD HILL LAMON (V.O.)
Mr. Lincoln pushed his Generals to
commence operations at once. They
met the enemy at Bull Run.

SOLDIERS (7) trudge by on Pennsylvania Ave; many bandaged,
limping, and leaning on their companions.

WARD HILL LAMON (V.O.)
It was a Union debacle.

43   INT. TELEGRAPH OFFICE - DAY   43

The control room of the Civil War. Ticking machines,
TELEGRAPHERS transcribing messages, and two giant maps
marking troop movements with blue and red pins: WESTERN
THEATER (MO, KY, TN, etc.) and EASTERN THEATER (VA, NC, SC,
etc.)

Lincoln and his Cabinet wait for someone. Lamon checks his
watch.

Finally, GEORGE McCLELLAN, 30's, mustached and Napoleonic,
strides in like the belle of the ball.

LINCOLN
General McClellan, you now command
all forces in the East. We outnum-
ber them two to one. I suggest we
advance everywhere at once - those
not skinning can hold a leg - and
the enemy will soon be overcome.

GENERAL MCCLELLAN
Mr. President, that is not the way
we conduct a war.

Everyone glances at Lincoln, to see if he's offended.

LINCOLN
Explain your plan.

With a supercilious manner, McClellan steps up to the Eastern
Theater map and starts concentrating blue pins in northern
Virginia.

Architectural element for the telegraph office where Lincoln spent so much of the war, awaiting news from his commanders.

Reading room, Carnegie Library and Music Hall, Allegheny City, Pennsylvania, Photographic print, ca. 1890, Library of Congress.

>   WARD HILL LAMON (V.O.)
>   *McClellan did transform our battered*
>   *eastern forces into a mighty army,*
>   *but he would not risk an actual*
>   *battle until he had more men,*
>   *cannon, and horses than Napoleon*
>   *himself. The result was stagnation*
>   *in the East, heavy losses in the*
>   *West, and mounting anger at Mr.*
>   *Lincoln.*

44   INT. LINCOLN'S OFFICE - DAY   44

Lincoln sits at his desk, sinking lower and lower as one
OFFICIAL after another berates him:

- Three ANGRY CONGRESSMEN.

>   COPPERHEAD DEMOCRAT
>   The people hate your war! They'll
>   not bleed for you or your beloved
>   Negroes! And you must stop now!

- Three ANGRY SENATORS led by SEN. CHARLES SUMNER, 50's, an
erudite firebrand.

>   SEN. CHARLES SUMNER
>   The people demand war! They want
>   the slaves freed! And you must act
>   now!

- And even Lincoln's own cabinet:

>   TREASURER CHASE
>   The war costs a million dollars a
>   day! We shall have to impose an
>   income tax to pay for it, and then
>   God help our Republican party.

>   SEC. OF STATE SEWARD
>   The lack of any success exasperates
>   Europe. They speak again of inter-
>   ceding. If that happens, we lose
>   all.

>   MONTGOMERY BLAIR
>   Are you not Commander-in-Chief? Do
>   something!

45   INT. WHITE HOUSE UPSTAIRS CORRIDOR - NIGHT   45

Lincoln sticks his head out of his office.

The East Room of the White House as it looked when Mary Todd Lincoln was First Lady.

Glass plate negative, wet collodion, Library of Congress.

                         LINCOLN
                    Hill!

46   INT. LINCOLN'S OFFICE - NIGHT   46

        Lamon replaces a string on his banjo. Lincoln paces.

                         LINCOLN
                    McClellan will not budge. The war's
                    end recedes into the far-off,
                    uncertain future like a mirage,
                    they all blame me-

                         WARD HILL LAMON
                    Did you not recently become
                    President?

                         LINCOLN
                    Hmph. I feel like that fellow who was
                    tarred and feathered and ridden out
                    of town on a rail. When someone in
                    the crowd asked how he liked it, he
                    replied-

                         WARD HILL LAMON
                    "If not for the honor of the thing, I
                    would much rather walk."

        They share a bittersweet laugh.

                         LINCOLN
                    Hill, I need a victory. Something
                    to show that the ship of state is
                    not in fact rudderless.

                         WARD HILL LAMON
                    I could visit McClellan - have a
                    talk, as I used to with our
                    recalcitrant clients.

                         LINCOLN
                    No, no, all account him a genius,
                    and he toils night and day
                    preparing the army for the great
                    battle to end this war. But I will
                    insist the other Generals advance.

47   INT. TELEGRAPH OFFICE - DAY   47

        Lincoln approaches MAJOR ECKERT, 30's, the chief telegrapher.

The Capitol dome was built during the Civil War - a testament to the nation's faith in a democratic and united future.

Salted paper print, between 1860 and 1863, Library of Congress.

                    MAJOR ECKERT
          Grant and Sherman are both moving
          in Kentucky, and Butler took the
          Outer Banks in North Carolina.

                    LINCOLN
          That is good!

                    MAJOR ECKERT
          We did have a setback at Balls
          Bluff.

                    LINCOLN
          Where is that?

                    MAJOR ECKERT
          Just up the river, sir. Small
          action, but a regiment was
          overwhelmed: 223 killed, including
          the commander... a Colonel Baker.

                    LINCOLN
          Ned Baker?!

                    MAJOR ECKERT
          It says Edward D. Baker.

Lincoln looks stricken.

                    MAJOR ECKERT (CONT'D)
          Did you know him, sir?

Lincoln nods, incapable of speaking.

48   INT. BAKER'S HOME - DAY   48

Baker lies in his casket. Lamon, Lincoln and Willie stand
with BAKER'S WIDOW and two grown CHILDREN.

                    LINCOLN
          Read your poem, son.

Willie, steps forward, unfolds a piece of paper and begins to
read, bravely fighting back tears.

                    WILLIE
          "There was no patriot like Baker,
          So noble and so true;
          He fell as a soldier on the field
          His face to the sky of blue."

Lincoln steps forward to comfort Willie.

Willie's eloquent poem eulogizing family friend Edward D. Baker was published in a local newspaper, the *Washington Republican*. Four months later, Willie too was dead.

Willie and Tad Lincoln, with their cousin
Lockwood Todd / Brady's National Portrait
Galleries, New York & Washington, 1861
Photographic print, albumen,
On carte de visite mount, Library of Congress.

Dear Sir:

I enclose you my first attempt at poetry.

Yours truly,
William W. Lincoln

> *There was no patriot like Baker,*
> *So noble and so true;*
> *He fell as a soldier on the field,*
> *His face to the sky of blue.*
>
> *His voice is silent in the hall,*
> *Which oft his presence grac'd.*
> *No more he'll hear the loud acclaim*
> *Which rang from place to place.*
>
> *No squeamish notions filled his breast,*
> *The Union was his theme;*
> *'No surrender and no compromise,'*
> *His day-thought and night's dream.*
>
> *His Country has her part to play,*
> *To'rd those he has left behind;*
> *His widow and his children all,*
> *She must always keep in mind.*

                    WILLIE (CONT'D)
          "His Country has her part to play,
          To'rd those he has left behind;
          His widow and his children all,
          She must always keep in mind."

                    LINCOLN
               (to Baker's corpse)
          I am so sorry, Ned.

49   INT. WHITE HOUSE PARLOUR - DAY   49

Lamon reviews a floor plan of the White House with four
DEPUTIES.

                    WARD HILL LAMON (V.O.)
          *Ned Baker was the only Senator ever
          to die in battle, and his death hit
          Washington hard.*

Lamon assigns a location to each man.

                    WARD HILL LAMON (V.O.)
          *Some weeks later, Mrs. Lincoln
          proposed a ball, to show that we
          remained confident of the war's
          outcome, and the President agreed.*

Lamon appoints an extra man to the front door.

                    WARD HILL LAMON (V.O.)
          *I was made Marshal of Ceremonies, a
          duty I often undertook to better
          control access to the President's
          person.*

51   INT. WILLIE'S BEDROOM - NIGHT   51

Band music can be heard. Willie lies in bed, feverish.

Mary kneels beside her son. She wears a silk ball gown. Mrs.
Keckly weaves flowers into her hair.

SUPER: FEBRUARY 5, 1862

Lincoln enters, also in formal wear.

                    LINCOLN
          The Marine band is playing, the
          banquet is served, and the only
          item lacking from the First Lady's
          Ball is the First Lady.

A composite image created from three separate images of the White House foyer and virtually relit for night. We used this image for the long tracking shot that encompasses three conversations at the First Lady's Ball.

                    WILLIE
              (raspy whisper)
          Go, Ma.

                    MARY
              (to Lincoln)
          I should've cancelled the ball.
          What if it's typhoid?

                    LINCOLN
          Dr. Stone said it's not.

                    MRS. KECKLY
          I have sat with many a sick child,
          Mrs. Lincoln. If the fever rises I
          will send for you.

                    LINCOLN
          Mother, Mrs. Keckly can be trusted.
          And we have 800 guests.

Mary kisses Willie and allows Lincoln to lead her away.

                    MARY
          There will be no dancing.

                    LINCOLN
          A ball with no dancing? Well, there
          is a war after all.

Lincoln continues soothing her as they leave, but he turns to
look back at his son, deeply concerned.

52   INT. WHITE HOUSE MAIN HALL - NIGHT   52

The mansion is filled with GUESTS in formal attire, standing
in small groups, drinking punch.

Mary converses with Sen. Charles Sumner, but she keeps
glancing up at the stairs.

                    MARY
          He is an abolitionist deep down,
          but his hands are tied.

                    SEN. CHARLES SUMNER
          It is not abolition. He is
          Commander-in-Chief of an army
          fighting a slave power.

Charles Sumner (1811-1874) was a United States Senator from
Massachusetts. He was a brilliant lawyer and orator, and a passionate
abolitionist. A close friend of Mary Lincoln, Senator Sumner was a
popular guest at the literary soirees she hosted at the White House.

Charles Sumner, between 1861 and 1874
Photographic print, Library of Congress.

                    MARY
              (distracted)
          Yes, free their slaves, and remove
          their power. I tell him repeatedly
          but he insists the cause is...

Across the room, Lincoln also glances at the stairs, while
conversing with Treasurer Chase.

                    LINCOLN
          ...Union. That is why our boys
          fight.

                    TREASURER CHASE
          What does our sacred Union stand
          for if not freedom?

                    LINCOLN
              (distracted)
          The border states are slave states.
          Any talk of emancipation will cause
          them to join the rebellion.

                    TREASURER CHASE
          Mr. President, doing God's will is
          more important than placating a pack
          of slave-holders at the border!

                    LINCOLN
          Mr. Chase, I would like to have God
          on my side, but I must have Kentucky.

In another part of the room, Marshal Lamon, wearing a silk
sash, chats with LUCILLE BOYD, 30's, a belle with flirty eyes
and ample décolletage. Both drink cocktails.

                    WARD HILL LAMON
          The honor is not ceremonial, Ma'am,
          I assure you. The President's life
          is in constant jeopardy.

                    LUCILLE BOYD
          How dreadful! And tell me, do you
          accompany him everywhere?

                    WARD HILL LAMON
          God knows I try, Ma'am, but he is a
          nimble gentleman.

                    LUCILLE BOYD
          Marshal Lamon, you are a Virginia
          horseman. How on earth could old
          Abe Lincoln escape your watch?

This photograph was used to create a military encampment on the streets of Washington DC in Scene 55. The script calls for us to see this from Lincoln's point of view, but in editing we decided to stay on Lincoln's face while seeing this image as a reflection in the window.

Atlanta, Ga. Trout House, Masonic Hall, and Federal encampment on Decatur Street, 1864
Glass plate negative, stereograph, wet collodion, Library of Congress.

                         WARD HILL LAMON
               Well, the War Department has many
               egresses and-

Lamon frowns. His eyes narrow.

                         WARD HILL LAMON (CONT'D)
               Ma'am, may I show you an
               astonishing sight?

                         LUCILLE BOYD
               Oh, please do.

He offers his arm, and she takes it. As he walks her toward
the front door, he catches the eye of his LEAD DEPUTY, 20's.

                         WARD HILL LAMON (V.O.)
               Washington swarmed with spies, many
               remarkably attractive. Extreme
               vigilance was required, even at the
               risk of discomforting the innocent.

53   EXT. WHITE HOUSE PORTICO - NIGHT   53

Lamon and his Deputy escort Lucille Boyd across the porch.

                         WARD HILL LAMON
               If I may?

He takes her cocktail.

                         WARD HILL LAMON (CONT'D)
                    (to Deputy)
               Old Cap Prison for interrogation.

                         LUCILLE BOYD
               But what have I done?!

                         WARD HILL LAMON
               We shall ask the questions, Ma'am.

As she leaves, he finishes her cocktail.

54   INT. WHITE HOUSE MAIN HALL - NIGHT   54

Lincoln and Mary converse with Sumner and two POLITICIANS.

Mrs. Keckly appears at the top of the stairs.

The Lincolns rush toward her.

This charming frame from *Saving Lincoln* becomes horrific when we hear Mary's bereaved screams in the distance. It is overwhelmingly white pursuant to our motif associating death with the ghostly white skies of Civil War photography, and our theme of making death meaningful. We believe there was a link between Willie's death and Lincoln's decision in the ensuing months to elevate the war's purpose from Union to Union-with-Emancipation.

55   INT. WILLIE'S BEDROOM - DAY   55

Days later. Willie looks terrible. Mary is worn out from crying. Mrs. Keckly bathes the boy's face with a towel.

By the window, Lincoln, unkempt and unshaven, talks with DR. STONE, 40's, a family physician.

> DR. STONE
> It is the war. The entire city is a
> barracks.

55A   EXT. LAFAYETTE SQUARE - DAY   55A

LINCOLN'S POV: Just outside the White House, a filthy encampment is visible.

> DR. STONE (O.S.)
> Gastric illness is widespread, and
> it often evolves into typhoid.

55B   INT. WILLIE'S BEDROOM - DAY   55B

Lincoln pales. Suddenly, Major Eckert rushes in with a telegraphic dispatch.

> MAJOR ECKERT
> Mr. President! From General Grant,
> sir.

> LINCOLN
> Yes?

> MAJOR ECKERT
> (reading)
> "I offered no terms but uncondi-
> tional and immediate surrender. Enemy
> accepted. Fort Donelson ours." It
> gives us the Cumberland River, sir. A
> true victory at last!

Lincoln gives Eckert a half-smile. Then Willie takes a pained, rattling breath. Lincoln rushes to the boy's side.

> LINCOLN
> Oh, dear God.

56   EXT. WHITE HOUSE - DAY   56

A great SHRIEK pierces the house.

This shot of children sledding in Central Park, NY had the perfect mood and hilly geography we were looking for as Lamon finds a shivering, bereaved Lincoln. To prep this photo for the film, our digital artists removed the human figures.

Coasting in Central Park, New York, between 1900 and 1906
Glass plate negative, Library of Congress.

57   INT. WILLIE'S BEDROOM - DAY   57

Lamon runs into Willie's room, just in time to see Mary fling
herself against the wall.

                         MARY
            AAAAAAAAGGGGHHHHH!!!!!!!

She BEATS the wall with her fists as Lamon and Mrs. Keckly
pull her away.

Willie's eyes are wide. Dr. Stone shuts them. Lincoln
squeezes the boy's hand.

                         LINCOLN
            My boy is gone. He is actually gone.
            Aaaaaagghhhh....

58   EXT. LAFAYETTE PARK - DAY   58

Sleet. Lincoln stands on a hilltop, coatless and soaked.

                    WARD HILL LAMON (V.O.)
            *When it is remembered that this
            calamity befell Mr. Lincoln during
            a period of the war when his mighty
            intellect was most in demand...*

Lamon spots Lincoln and hustles over.

                    WARD HILL LAMON (V.O.)
            *...it will be understood that
            within a few short weeks his
            incapacity became a matter of grave
            concern to the entire government.*

Lamon takes off his own coat and wraps it around the
President, then drags him toward the White House.

59   INT. WHITE HOUSE VESTIBULE - DAY   59

Wilting funeral wreaths crowd the foyer. Tables, mirrors and
windows are draped in black. Lamon leads the sopping
President toward the stairs.

                    IMPATIENT VOICES
            Mr. President!

Three men converge on Lincoln: John Hay, Sec. of State
Seward, and EDWIN STANTON, 47, long beard, fierce eyes,
utterly competent and authoritarian.

Lincoln showed great mercy to young deserters he called "my leg cases" - "If Almighty God gives a man a cowardly pair of legs, how can he help their running away with him?"

This scene was omitted from *Saving Lincoln* for reasons of pace. In the script, we meet Secretary of War Stanton for the first time, and he tells Lincoln that McClellan finally moved forward only to learn that the Confederate fortifications (which had held him back for so long) were actually logs painted to look like cannon, i.e. "Quaker guns."

Centreville, Virginia. Confederate fort with Quaker gun
March, 1862
Glass plate negative, wet collodion, Library of Congress.

                    SEC. OF WAR STANTON
          McClellan finally advanced, only to
          find the enemy gone and a row of
          logs painted to look like cannon!

                    LINCOLN
               (dazed)
          Yes...?

                    SEC. OF WAR STANTON
          All these months of stalling, and
          we never were outnumbered, Mr.
          President! We are made ridiculous,
          sir, and you must sack him!

                    LINCOLN
          But he advanced...?

                    SEC. OF STATE SEWARD
          Mr. President, General Butler has
          announced publicly that slaves
          running across our lines will be
          treated as contraband of war.

                    LINCOLN
          Contraband...?

                    SEC. OF STATE SEWARD
          Meaning he will no longer return
          them to their owners, even in the
          border states. You must overrule
          him, sir, distasteful as that may
          be, or lose those crucial states to
          the rebellion!

                    LINCOLN
          I must...I mean, I cannot...

                    HAY
               (presenting a document)
          Mr. President, this boy ran off
          from the 7th New York. He will be
          shot in the morning unless you sign
          the pardon.

Lincoln leans forward to sign, and loses his balance. Lamon
steadies him so he can scrawl his name.

                    SEC. OF WAR STANTON
          I object, sir! Every time you
          pardon one of these cowards for
          deserting, you encourage another!

We used this plate for Scene 60. Lamon often soothed Lincoln's troubled soul, thus enabling him to work. After Willie's death, however, even Lamon could not ease Lincoln's melancholy.

Residence of Dr. J.H. Lancashire, Alma, Mich., between 1900-1910
Glass plate negative, Library of Congress.

When Willie died, Tad was also gravely ill with typhoid.
Tad Lincoln, Carte de visite
Library of Congress.

                    WARD HILL LAMON
          Suh, you must desist. He is not
          well, and these matters will wait.

                    SEC. OF WAR STANTON
          They will not wait - the nation is
          at stake!

But Lamon hustles Lincoln away.

60   INT. LINCOLN'S DRESSING ROOM - NIGHT   60

Lincoln wears a robe. He sits listless, with his bare feet in
a basin to which Lamon adds steaming water.

                    WARD HILL LAMON
          When I lost my wife, you covered my
          cases as long as I needed. But God
          help me, Lincoln, I cannot cover
          yours. You must-

Lincoln suddenly gets up and walks out, still barefoot.

61   INT. TAD'S ROOM - NIGHT   61

Eyes closed, Tad lies on his bed, holding the doll, Jack.
After a long beat, he breathes.

Lincoln stands over him. He looks relieved. Hear a FOOTSTEP.
Lincoln turns.

Mrs. Keckly stands just inside the doorway.

                    LINCOLN
          How is Mrs. Lincoln?

                    MRS. KECKLY
          She is prostrated, Mr. President,
          and I am very concerned. Her
          anguish destroys her. She blames
          herself for Willie's... because the
          ball was so lavish.

                    LINCOLN
          Perhaps she is right. I should not
          have allowed it.

                    MRS. KECKLY
          Oh no, sir! No! The Lord took
          Willie for His own purposes.

                    LINCOLN
          An eleven year old boy? What
          purpose was that?

                              40.

Approximately 180,000 African-American men served in the U.S. Army during the Civil War, comprising 10% of the Union Army. One third of all black soldiers died, most of them from disease. They were paid $10 a month, unlike white soldiers, who made $13.

Arlington, Va. Band of 107th U.S. Colored Infantry at Fort Corcoran, 1865
Glass plate negative, wet collodion, Library of Congress.

Lamon watches them from another doorway.

                    MRS. KECKLY
          I'm sorry, sir. I did not mean to-

                    LINCOLN
          Tell me, Mrs. Keckly. What purpose
          had God to take my son?

                    MRS. KECKLY
          I...I cannot say, sir. But when I
          lost my son, I was comforted by the
          story of Jacob. He mourned for
          Joseph all those years, yet in the
          end, it was because Joseph was taken
          that he became God's instrument in
          saving the whole family.

                    LINCOLN
          But Joseph was not dead!

                    MRS. KECKLY
          No, sir, and neither is Willie. He
          lives in Paradise.

                    LINCOLN
          "Lives?!" Would that I had your
          faith, Mrs. Keckly. For I have lost
          many people. Another son years ago.
          My sister. My mother when I was a
          boy. Others are comforted by
          stories of heaven, but I have never
          had that faculty.

                    MRS. KECKLY
          Beg pardon, sir, but faith is not a
          faculty. It is a choice. No one can
          prove that God is, or is not. Yet
          anyone can choose to seek His wisdom,
          and His mercy, in this world. When I
          made that choice, I began to see His
          purpose, even in our sufferings, and
          that choice has sustained me through
          terrible days, sir.

In his doorway, still unseen, Lamon nods.

                    LINCOLN
          When did you lose your son, Mrs.
          Keckly?

                    MRS. KECKLY
          Last year, at Wilson's Creek.

"If I had had my way, this war would never have been commenced; if I had been allowed my way this war would have ended before this, but we find it still continues; and we must believe that He permits it for some wise purpose of His own, mysterious and unknown to us; and though with our limited understandings we may not be able to comprehend it, yet we cannot but believe, that He who made the world still governs it."

- Abraham Lincoln, October 26, 1862

                         LINCOLN
          The Battle of Wilson's Creek?

                         MRS. KECKLY
          Yes, sir. George was a light-
          skinned boy, and he could pass. He
          enlisted as soon as the war began.

                         LINCOLN
          In an army that would not have
          taken him if his race were known...
          Mrs. Keckly, I am so very sorry.
          George was a true patriot.

                         MRS. KECKLY
          He enlisted to fight slavery, sir.
          George and I were both slaves until
          1855. It took me thirty years to
          purchase our freedom with the money
          I earned dress-making. But the Lord
          heard our cries, Mr. President, the
          cries of my people, and He
          remembered us, and He sent you to
          deliver us.

                         LINCOLN
          Mrs. Keckly, no! I am no prophet - I
          am just a man, of the commonest
          sort, I assure you.

                         MRS. KECKLY
          If that is true, sir, then how did
          you come to be President?

                         LINCOLN
          Why, I...

She grasps Lincoln's hands.

                         MRS. KECKLY
          Mr. President, trust God. You are
          His instrument, sir, and you will
          do His work. With Willie watching
          over you.

She hastily kisses his hands, and turns to leave. She passes
Lamon, who lurks in the doorway, watching.

Lamon's POV: Ever so slowly, the President brings his hands
together in prayer. Sobbing, he drops to his knees.

Abraham Lincoln's Preliminary Emancipation Proclamation.

Busy hubbub as Major Eckert and other telegraph operators jot down their dispatches on foolscap paper.

Perched at a tiny desk in the corner, Lincoln writes with a dip pen:

"...I, Abraham Lincoln, as President of the United States"

Lincoln pauses, then rewrites:

"I, Abraham Lincoln, ~~President of the United States~~ as Commander-in-Chief of the Army and Navy..."

Lincoln mutters the words to himself. Satisfied, he writes:

"do order and declare that all persons held as slaves in any rebellious state"

Lincoln pauses again, takes a breath, and writes:

"shall be free."

> MAJOR ECKERT
> Mr. President! Dispatch from
> General Grant.

Lincoln looks up. Stanton runs in to hear it.

> MAJOR ECKERT (CONT'D)
> (reading)
> "From Shiloh Church on the
> Tennessee River... driven back
> yesterday... regrouped,
> counterattacked, and held the
> river." Sir, it is a great victory!

> SEC. OF WAR STANTON
> Hallelujah!

Lincoln's look: an emphatic "yes."

> MAJOR ECKERT
> "...especially commend General
> Sherman for holding the center
> though wounded twice, and three
> horses shot out from under him!"

> SEC. OF WAR STANTON
> Give that to the papers. We need a
> hero.

Scene 63 Storyboard - EXT. 7TH STREET PIKE - NIGHT
This scene was one of our greatest CineCollage challenges. We thought the
toughest part would be bringing horses onto our green screen stage, but
they turned out to be experienced actors who welcomed the challenge. More
difficult was assembling our forest plates into a 3D environment through
which the horses could move.

                    LINCOLN
          And the casualties?

                    MAJOR ECKERT
          Uhhh...

He receives a dispatch from another Telegrapher.

                    MAJOR ECKERT (CONT'D)
          Oh. Dear God. 13,000.

                    LINCOLN
          That is both sides???

                    MAJOR ECKERT
          Union, sir. The enemy lost 10,000.

Lincoln puts down his pen, his face ashen.

                    LINCOLN
          Just to hold a piece of river...

                    SEC. OF WAR STANTON
          Losing 13,000 to their 10 is not
          "winning." Grant must be replaced,
          sir.

                    LINCOLN
          I cannot spare this man. He fights.

63   EXT. 7TH STREET PIKE - NIGHT   63

A mounted Lamon GALLOPS up a semi-rural road in the
moonlight, desperately urging his horse to go faster.

                    WARD HILL LAMON (V.O.)
          Mr. Lincoln had resumed his duties,
          but not his routine. Hoping to ease
          Mary's grief, he shifted his family
          to the Summer Residence.

Lamon spots Lincoln's unmistakable silhouette ahead.

                    WARD HILL LAMON
          The result was a daily, three-mile
          ride along an unguarded road
          teeming with opportunities for
          ambush - a trip he often undertook
          without notice to me.

Lamon finally catches up and glares fiercely at Lincoln, but
Lincoln is lost in thought and barely glances back.

While these organic lawn mowers worked outside, Lincoln astounded his Cabinet with his Emancipation Proclamation, thus changing course in the middle of the war.

White House. Sheep on lawn, between 1916 and 1919
Glass plate negative, Library of Congress.

Lamon settles into guard duty, scanning their surroundings for trouble.

Something moves in the trees. Lamon stands in his stirrups.

Someone WHISPERS.

                    WARD HILL LAMON (CONT'D)
               (drawing his revolvers)
          Show yourself!

SCAMPERING in the bushes. Lamon FIRES in the air.

                    WARD HILL LAMON (CONT'D)
          I am a U.S. Marshal, and I will
          shoot you!

FOOTSTEPS recede quickly as someone runs away. Unconcerned, Lincoln jots a note in the margin of a document.

Lamon looks at Lincoln and shakes his head in consternation.

64   INT. LINCOLN'S OFFICE - DAY   64

Document in hand, Lincoln stands before his Cabinet.

SUPER: JULY 22, 1862

                    LINCOLN
               (reading aloud)
          "I, as Commander-in-Chief of the
          Army and Navy of the United States,
          do order and declare that on the
          1st of January, 1863, all persons
          held as slaves within any state
          wherein the Constitutional
          Authority of the United States
          shall not be recognized and
          submitted to, shall then, thence-
          forward, and forever, be free."

He puts down the paper and looks around him.

                    MONTGOMERY BLAIR
          You have changed your mind entirely.

                    LINCOLN
          Yes I have, Mr. Blair, and I don't
          think much of a man who is not
          wiser today than he was yesterday.
          Gentlemen, who's for it?

Lincoln and Sec. of War Stanton raise their hands. Lincoln stares at Treasurer Chase, who looks away.

45.

First Reading of the Emancipation Proclamation of President Lincoln.

Shown from left to right are:

      Edwin M. Stanton, Secretary of War (seated);
      Salmon P. Chase, Secretary of the Treasury (standing);
      Abraham Lincoln, President of the United States (seated);
      Gideon Welles, Secretary of the Navy (seated);
      Caleb Blood Smith, Secretary of the Interior (standing);
      William H. Seward, Secretary of State (seated);
      Montgomery Blair, Postmaster General (standing);
      Edward Bates, Attorney General (seated).

Painting by Francis Bicknell Carpenter
Engraved by Alexander Hay Ritchie, 1866
Library of Congress.

                    LINCOLN (CONT'D)
          Against?

Monty Blair raises his hand, followed by Sec. of State Seward
and slowly, Chase.

                    LINCOLN (CONT'D)
          The ayes have it.

                    TREASURER CHASE
          But the vote was three to two.

                    LINCOLN
          Mr. Chase, I am knocked into a
          cocked hat to hear you disapprove
          of this measure.

                    TREASURER CHASE
          I favor emancipation, of course,
          but to do it now, when we must pass
          an income tax and sell war bonds-

                    SEC. OF WAR STANTON
          You would prefer to wait until
          1864? Allow the next President to
          free the slaves? Perhaps you?

                    TREASURER CHASE
          I believe it would be better to
          organize and arm the slaves.

                    LINCOLN
          No, it would not. But we will accept
          Negroes into the armed forces.

                    SEC. OF WAR STANTON
          Hear hear!

Lincoln jots a note on the document.

                    SEC. OF STATE SEWARD
          Mr. President, issuing this
          proclamation now, with the
          Rebellion completely unchecked,
          might well be deemed the last,
          desperate shriek of an exhausted
          government.

                    TREASURER CHASE
          Precisely.

                    SEC. OF STATE SEWARD
          It's the wrong message to send
          Europe.

John Wilkes Booth made his acting debut in Richard III in 1855. When he finally played the title role in 1862, he explained his natural inclination for the role by saying, "I am determined to be a villain."

Lincoln nods, comprehending.

>   SEC. OF STATE SEWARD (CONT'D)
>   I approve the measure, you know my
>   views, but I strongly recommend we
>   postpone the Emancipation
>   Proclamation-

>   LINCOLN
>   Until we win a battle.

>   SEC. OF STATE SEWARD
>   Just so.

66   INT. ILLINOIS STATEHOUSE - NIGHT - **FLASH FORWARD**   66

Lamon speaks in the dark Statehouse.

>   WARD HILL LAMON
>   Months passed without our winning
>   so much as a skirmish. For relief,
>   Mr. Lincoln turned to theater-
>   going, a practice I vehemently
>   opposed for bringing him so near to
>   great mobs in darkened rooms.

Reveal that Lamon stands before Lincoln's open casket.

>   WARD HILL LAMON (O.S.) (CONT'D)
>   I always feared that some villain
>   would level his pistol at my
>   friend, though I never imagined the
>   malefactor might be standing upon
>   the stage itself.

67   INT. THEATER - NIGHT   67

Start on a handbill that reads "William Shakespeare's Richard
III." Above the title of the play, we see the name of its
star, "John Wilkes Booth!"

>   NOBLE #1 (O.S.)
>   Would you imagine, the subtle
>   traitor this day had plotted in the
>   council house to murder me and my
>   good Lord of Gloster?...

Keep rising to reveal Lincoln and Tad mesmerized by a play.

>   NOBLE #2 (O.S.)
>   What, had he so?

To create the scenes where Lincoln and Lamon are riding in a carriage, our team created a virtual "rolling backdrop," sewn together from dozens of images in multiple layers of depth. Some of those images are shown here.

LINCOLN'S POV: on the stage, JOHN WILKES BOOTH, 26, a handsome star now playing a crippled usurper, converses with two NOBLES, one of whom carries a <u>severed head</u>.

> JOHN WILKES BOOTH
> "What?! Think you we are Turks or infidels? Or that we would, against the form of law, proceed thus rashly with the villain's death...

LINCOLN'S POV: Booth glares directly at us.

> JOHN WILKES BOOTH (CONT'D)
> ...but that the extreme peril of the case, the peace of England, and our person's safety enforced us to this execution?!"

> TAD
> (to Lincoln, amused)
> He looks as if he meant that for you, Papa!

> LINCOLN
> He does look at me pretty sharp, doesn't he?

Reveal Lamon standing behind Lincoln, looking not at the play but at the audience.

> WARD HILL LAMON (V.O.)
> *Would that I had seen that look, but at the time, John Wilkes Booth was only one of a multitude looking sharply at our President.*

69   EXT. MARYLAND ROAD - DAY   69

Lincoln and Lamon ride in a carriage.

> WARD HILL LAMON (V.O.)
> *McClellan had finally provided the long-awaited victory.*

Lincoln reads a newspaper, Lamon scans their surroundings.

> WARD HILL LAMON (V.O.)
> *The Proclamation was made public, and death threats to Mr. Lincoln increased by a hundredfold.*

Lamon glances at an official-looking paper and scowls.

"Fellow-citizens, we cannot escape history. We of this Congress and this administration, will be remembered in spite of ourselves. No personal significance, or insignificance, can spare one or another of us. The fiery trial through which we pass, will light us down, in honor or dishonor, to the latest generation."
- Abraham Lincoln, 1862

                    WARD HILL LAMON (V.O.)
          One syndicate of Georgia planters
          even issued a bond worth $50,000
          for my friend's life, and I could
          never know who would be tempted by
          such a vast offer.

The carriage rolls into the outskirts of an Army encampment.
Lamon glares all around, suspicious of everyone.

SOLDIERS notice the President's arrival. Some salute. Many do
not. Lincoln tips his hat to every one.

                    LINCOLN
          Good morning boys. Bless you, son.
          Thank you for your service...

                    SOLDIER GRINDING COFFEE
          Didn't sign up to free no darkies.

The soldier spits. Lamon stares daggers at him.

                    LINCOLN
          Thank you for your great service. I
          am in your debt.

70   EXT. BATTLEFIELD - DAY   70

Lincoln and McClellan face each other stiffly while posing
for a PHOTOGRAPHER's camera.

Also in the shot are several ARMY OFFICERS (6). Lamon is
included too, but seated off to the side.

                    MCCLELLAN
          Dunker church, Burnside bridge...
          and that is Bloody Lane, where I
          pierced the Confederate center.

                    LINCOLN
          Herded them from the field of
          honor, eh?

                    MCCLELLAN
          Like sheep, Mr. President.

                    LINCOLN
          Why then did you not pursue? The
          bleating sheep were before you, the
          axe in your hand. You might have
          crushed Lee's army and ended this
          terrible contest.

Lincoln and McClellan. The tension speaks for itself. This famous photograph of President Lincoln visiting General McClellan at Antietam is re-enacted in *Saving Lincoln*, and includes photographer Alexander Gardner. It's an awkward moment for President and General - they must pause their heated argument for 10 seconds while the photographer exposes the plate.

President Lincoln with Gen. George B. McClellan and officers (detail)
Antietam, MD, October 3, 1862
Glass plate negative, wet collodion, Library of Congress.

                    MCCLELLAN
          Why, we were exhausted. The
          fighting-

                    LINCOLN
          How many thousands more will perish
          because you let him fly?

                    MCCLELLAN
          I repelled Lee's invasion, sir!

                    PHOTOGRAPHER
          Hold still, please, and 1,2,3,4,5...

Lincoln and McClellan glare at each other during the long
exposure time required by 19th century photography.

                    PHOTOGRAPHER (CONT'D)
          ...6,7,8,9,10. Thank you, gentlemen.

                    MCCLELLAN
               (to Lincoln)
          And I did it no thanks to you or
          any other politician!

But Lincoln is already walking away.

                    WARD HILL LAMON (V.O.)
          *General McClellan was finally
          relieved of his command.*

71   EXT. MARYLAND ROAD - DAY   71

Lincoln and Lamon ride by a burnt-out church in another part
of the battlefield.

They pass row after row after row of crude grave markers.
Lincoln stares at the graves with a pained expression.

Finally, they leave the graves behind.

                    LINCOLN
          Hill, sing that sad song.

Lamon looks reluctant, but he pulls out his banjo and begins:

                    WARD HILL LAMON
               (singing)
          *I've wandered to the village, Tom,
          I've sat beneath the tree,*

Lincoln's eyes look far away and despondent.

"Twenty Years Ago" was Lincoln's favorite mournful ballad. Here are the complete lyrics:

I've wandered to the village, Tom
I've sat beneath the tree
Upon the schoolhouse playing ground
Which sheltered you and me
But none were there to greet me, Tom
And few were left to know
That played with us upon the grass
Some twenty years ago

The grass is just as green, dear Tom
Barefooted boys at play
Were sporting just as we did then
With spirits just as gay
But the Master sleeps upon the hill
Which coated, o'er with snow
Afforded us a sliding place
Just twenty years ago

The river's running just as still
The willows on its side
Are larger than they were, dear Tom
The stream appears less wide
The grapevine swing is ruined now
Where once we played the beau
And swung our sweethearts "pretty girls"
Just twenty years ago

The spring that bubbled 'neath the hill
Close by the spreading beech
Is very low; 'twas once so high
That we could almost reach
And kneeling down to get a drink
Dear Tom, I started so
To see how much that I was changed
Since twenty years ago

Near by the spring, upon an elm
You know I cut your name
Your sweetheart's just beneath it, Tom
And you did mine the same
Some heartless wretch had peeled the bark
'Twas dying sure but slow
Just as that one, whose name was cut
Died twenty years ago

My lids have long been dry, dear Tom
But tears came in my eyes
I thought of her I loved so well
Those early-broken ties
I visited the old churchyard
And took some flowers to strew
Upon the graves of those we loved
Some twenty years ago

Some now are in the churchyard laid
Some sleep beneath the sea
But few are left of our old class
Excepting you and me
And when our time shall come, dear Tom
And we are called to go
I hope they'll lay us where we played
Just twenty years ago

> WARD HILL LAMON (CONT'D)
> *But none were there to greet me,*
> *Tom, and few were left to know,*
> *That played with us upon the green,*
> *some twenty years ago—*

Seeing Lincoln's despair, Lamon suddenly starts singing a new, jolly tune:

> WARD HILL LAMON (CONT'D)
> *Now here I am a going to sing,*
> *And tell you how the banjo'll ring,*
> *This song I know't please you to death,*
> *An laugh you nearly out of breath!*

Lincoln forces a smile, acknowledging Lamon's efforts to cheer him, but he's too depressed to join in.

> WARD HILL LAMON (CONT'D)
> *Picayune, Butler, comin', comin'...*

72   EXT. PENNSYLVANIA AVENUE - DAY   72

Lamon strides along singing softly.

> WARD HILL LAMON
> *Picayune, Butler, come to town...*

He passes a NEWSPAPER SELLER and buys a paper. The headline says, "Scandal! President Mocks the Fallen!"

> WARD HILL LAMON (CONT'D)
> (reading)
> "...day after the battle...dead
> soldiers heaped by the roadside...
> Lincoln slapped the knee of Marshal
> Lamon and exclaimed, 'Give us that
> song about Picayune Butler!'"

Aghast, Lamon runs toward the White House.

73   INT. TAD'S ROOM - DAY   73

Lamon runs in as Lincoln and Tad act out a scene with paper dolls in Tad's toy theater. Lincoln's doll is a man with a donkey head.

> LINCOLN
> "Methinks I am marvelous hairy
> about the face!"

> WARD HILL LAMON
> Suh! I am aggrieved!

51.

The unfinished Washington Monument as it stood during the Civil War.
Glass plate negative, wet collodion, Library of Congress.

                    LINCOLN
          "And I am such a tender ass, if my hair
          do but tickle me, I must scratch!"

Tad doubles over laughing. Lincoln enjoys the boy's happiness.

                    WARD HILL LAMON
          The papers have attacked you on my
          account - the song I sang, near the
          battlefield-

                    LINCOLN
          I know, Hill.

                    WARD HILL LAMON
          I shall resign.

                    LINCOLN
          You committed no wrong. If my
          character is not sufficiently
          established to give the lie to such
          reports, then I am much mistaken as
          to the people's regard for this
          administration. Now, Tadpole, what
          part shall Marshal Lamon play?

                    TAD
          Robin Goodfellow!

                    LINCOLN
          Robin Goodfellow it is!

Lincoln hands Lamon a paper doll.

                    WARD HILL LAMON (V.O.)
          My friend stood by me, but he was
          mistaken as to the people's regard
          for his administration. In the mid-
          term elections which soon followed,
          we lost 50 seats in the Congress,
          and the political assassination of
          Abraham Lincoln began in earnest.

74   EXT. WASHINGTON MONUMENT - DAY   74

Sound of RIFLE FIRE. At a target range near the uncompleted
Washington Monument, Lincoln and an INVENTOR test the new
"repeating rifles." Lamon has to shout over the noise.

                    WARD HILL LAMON
          You do not appreciate the danger, suh!

BANG! Lincoln fires his rifle.

We are proud to count actual Civil War veterans among our actors in *Saving Lincoln* - we include them as photographic extras. We share additional pictures of Civil War soldiers every week on Remembrance Thursday at Facebook.com/SavingLincoln.

Patients in Ward K of Armory Square Hospital, Washington, D.C., 1865
Glass plate negative, wet collodion, Library of Congress.

                    WARD HILL LAMON (CONT'D)
          Senators Wade, Davis, Pomeroy -
          even Sumner by his silence - they
          all conspire against you!

                    LINCOLN
          Hill, for a man of accredited
          courage, you are the most panicky
          person I know.

                    WARD HILL LAMON
          They call you indecisive, feeble,
          incapable of winning the war...

BANG! Lincoln fires again.

                    LINCOLN
          Hill, criticism is not conspiracy.

                    WARD HILL LAMON
          Can you not see they maneuver to
          replace you on the Republican slate?

BANG!

                    LINCOLN
          I do. So I think we'd better win
          the war before November '64.
                    (to Inventor)
          Mr. Spencer, we'll take 10,000.

75   INT. HOSPITAL - DAY   75

       Attended by Lamon, Lincoln walks down a hospital ward,
       offering Presidential thanks to amputees.

                    WARD HILL LAMON (V.O.)
          *But the new rifles did not alleviate
          our long season of failures. 1863
          arrived, and with it, more loss.*

       PRIVATE DYER, a young soldier missing his right arm, offers
       his left hand to the President.

                    LINCOLN
          Deeply grateful for your service.

75A   INT. OPERATING ROOM - DAY   75A

       Lincoln and Lamon walk into an operating area.

       Three MEN hold down a PRIVATE. The poor boy has already lost
       his right arm. Now the SURGEON begins to amputate his left
       with a bloody saw.

                              53.

Wet collodion photography required immense amounts of light so there are relatively few indoor plates. This kitchen became our operating room, which is appropriate because Civil War hospitals were often overwhelmed and soldiers received treatment under any roof available.

Cooks in the kitchen of Soldiers' Rest, Alexandria, VA, 1865
Glass plate negative, wet collodion, Library of Congress.

Lamon cannot watch. Lincoln forces himself.

77   EXT. WHITE HOUSE - DAY   77

Sunset. Still shaken, Lincoln and Lamon walk toward the White
House.

Treasurer Chase walks by and tips his hat cheerfully.

                    TREASURER CHASE
          Good evening, Mr. President!

                    LINCOLN
          Uh? Oh, yes.

Lincoln tips his hat but Chase is already past. Lincoln and
Lamon walk up the White House driveway.

                    LINCOLN (CONT'D)
          Perhaps Chase should be President.
          He always seems to know what the
          Almighty wants. Whereas I... I
          thought for one moment I was God's
          instrument, and then I brought down
          nothing but misery and despair.

                    WARD HILL LAMON
          Nothing but misery and...?

Lamon turns to his friend and grasps his arms.

                    WARD HILL LAMON (CONT'D)
          Come with me.

78   EXT. CITY STREET - NIGHT   78

Lincoln and Lamon reach an encampment of African-American
FREEDMEN, crowded together with their few belongings. A small
group (5) sings around a fire.

                    GOSPEL SINGERS
          If I could I surely would,
          Stand on the rock where Moses stood...
          Pharaoh's army got drownded,
          Oh Mary don't you weep.
          O Mary, don't you weep, don't you mourn
          O Mary, don't you weep, don't you mourn
          Pharaoh's army got drownded
          O Mary, don't you weep!

SCENE 78

Recently freed slaves poured into
Washington DC. Elizabeth Keckly and
Mary Lincoln coordinated relief drives
for them, collecting food and clothing
from wealthy society ladies.

A small group of freedmen sang gospel
songs for spare change just a few blocks
from the White House.

                    WARD HILL LAMON
                 (to Lincoln)
          These people escaped because you
          proclaimed them free. Here is no
          misery, suh. Here is hope.

Watching the singers, Lincoln's face begins to soften.

The Freedmen notice Lincoln and stop singing. Amazed, they
start to touch him, as if to ensure he is real. An Elderly
Freedman begins to kneel.

                    LINCOLN
          God bless you. Please don't kneel
          before me. My heart is with you.
          Bless you, my dear. Please, sing!
          You sound wonderful. Sing!

                    GOSPEL SINGERS
          Oh Mary don't you weep, don't you
          moan...

Lincoln and Lamon join in and the music <u>swells powerfully</u>:

                    LINCOLN & GOSPEL SINGERS
          Pharaoh's army got drownded,
          Oh Mary don't you weep...

                    ELDERLY FREEMAN
          When I get to heaven, gonna scream
          and shout... nobody there gonna put
          me out!

                    LINCOLN & GOSPEL SINGERS
          Pharaoh's army got drownded,
          Oh Mary don't you weep...

All are ebullient, even Lincoln.

                    WARD HILL LAMON (V.O.)
          July 4, 1863. For a moment, we
          thought the war had ended.

79   INT. TELEGRAPH OFFICE - DAY   79

Lincoln and the rest of the Cabinet clap each other on the
back as Sec. of War Stanton pulls red pins off the "Western
Theater" map. An "Eastern Theater" map hangs beside it.

                    WARD HILL LAMON (V.O.)
          In the West, Grant captured
          Vicksburg at last, and an entire
          army with it.
                        (MORE)

                            55.

We used this home as a facsimile of the Soldiers' Home, also known as the Lincolns' Summer Residence. Lincoln's daily commute to the White House, often unguarded, was a source of great vexation to Lamon.

Residence of John Minor Botts. (Family on porch), Culpeper, VA, 1863
Glass plate negative, wet collodion, Library of Congress.

                    WARD HILL LAMON (V.O.) (CONT'D)
          And in the East, where General Lee
          had invaded Pennsylvania...

Major Eckert jumps up from his desk with a dispatch.

                    MAJOR ECKERT
          From General Meade at Gettysburg:
          "We have driven the invader from
          our soil!"

All the Cabinet men rejoice. Lincoln, however, simply grabs
the dispatch from Eckert.

                    LINCOLN
          "Driven the invader from our soil?"
          My God, is that all?!

                    MAJOR ECKERT
          Yes, sir.

                    LINCOLN
          Lee was two states away from his base
          of supply - Meade could've captured
          his entire army!

                    SEC. OF STATE SEWARD
          But sir, we won the battle.

                    LINCOLN
          And lost 23,000 men! 23,000 killed,
          mangled, missing, and Lee right back
          where he was! The People won't stand
          for it. They will demand peace at any
          price, and then all of this...

Lincoln rips both maps from the wall.

                    LINCOLN (CONT'D)
          ...is for nothing! NOTHING!

No one dares speak as Lincoln catches his breath.

Lamon suddenly enters. He rushes to Lincoln's side.

                    WARD HILL LAMON
          Mr. President! Something has
          happened to Mrs. Lincoln.

80   EXT. SUMMER RESIDENCE - DAY   80

Lincoln and Lamon rush from their horses toward a Victorian
cottage.

SUPER: THE PRESIDENT'S SUMMER RESIDENCE

To place the actors inside photographs like these, our camera crew had
to match the lighting of the original photo. A large amount of daylight
pours into this room from behind camera. We duplicated that look on
set, and ended with a very bright, almost washed out look that added an
ominous intensity to Mary's distress.

Bedroom in the White House, Washington, D.C., 1893
Photographic print, Library of Congress.

Mary lies in bed delirious, her head wrapped in bandages.
Mrs. Keckly steps aside as Lincoln rushes in.

                    MRS. KECKLY
          The driver's bench fell off the
          carriage! The horses ran... Oh,
          sir, this was a terrible accident!

                    WARD HILL LAMON
               (to Lincoln)
          This was no accident, suh. A killer
          loosed that bench, in the hopes
          that you would be the passenger.

Lincoln sits beside Mary and takes her hand.

                    LINCOLN
          Mother. Is the pain great?

                    MARY
          Yes. Yet I do not mind it, for
          Nettie brings me such comfort.

                    LINCOLN
          Nettie?

                    MRS. KECKLY
          Nettie Colburn, sir, the medium.
          She is famously gifted.

Lamon frowns.

                    MARY
          I have spoken to Willie, Father. He
          is so happy in Heaven.

                    LINCOLN
          Is he.

                    MARY
          Yes, yes! As are Sam, and little
          Aleck. Did you know they fell at
          Baton Rouge and Shiloh?

                    LINCOLN
          Of course, Mother.

                    MARY
          I could not mourn my own brothers,
          lest the papers call me a traitor.
          But now they know how much I miss
          them. Especially Willie, father.
                    (MORE)

SCENE 83

SCENE 85

SCENE 84

"It is now an acknowledged fact that there never was a moment from the day [Mr. Lincoln] crossed the Maryland line up to the time of his assassination that he was not in danger of death by violence, and that his life was spared until the night of the 14th of April 1865 only through the ceaseless and watchful care of the guards thrown around him."

- Ward Hill Lamon, *Recollections of Abraham Lincoln*

                    MARY (CONT'D)
          He comes to me now, even without
          Nettie's help. The little rascal.

                    LINCOLN
          I am glad he is...well.

                    MARY
          Will you not attend a séance with
          me, Father? Nettie summons others
          from beyond, some wondrously wise.
          They can help you win the war.

                    LINCOLN
          I will, Mother, as soon as my
          schedule permits. You rest now, and
          we will all dote on you until your
          wounds are healed.

82   INT. HALLWAY - DAY   82

Lincoln leads Lamon out of Mary's room.

                    LINCOLN
          Find them.

83   EXT. TOWNHOUSE - NIGHT   83

Lamon KNOCKS on the door of a Georgetown home.

84   INT. GEORGETOWN PUB - NIGHT   84

Lamon's Deputies pull a SUSPECT away from his table.

85   INT. OLD CAPITAL PRISON - NIGHT   85

Deputies bring two handcuffed SUSPECTS to the jailhouse from
different directions.

86   EXT/INT. TOWNHOUSE - NIGHT   86

Lamon KNOCKS insistently on the townhouse door. An ELEGANT
MAN opens it.

                    ELEGANT MAN
          Good evening.

                    WARD HILL LAMON
          Evening, sir. Ward Hill Lamon, U.S.
          Marshal. We are investigating an
          attempted...

Lamon looks past the man into the townhouse. He sees Lucille
Boyd, <u>the flirty belle he arrested at the ball</u>.

Any time we drive past an old cemetery, we stop and walk among the departed. We always seek out the military markers, paying our respects, and silently honoring these veterans for their service.

Soldiers' Cemetery, Alexandria, VA, between 1861 and 1869
Glass plate negative, wet collodion, Library of Congress.

                    WARD HILL LAMON (CONT'D)
                  (pulling his pistols)
               I arrest you both!

89   INT. HOTEL - NIGHT   89

        Lamon leads his Deputy into a hotel room.

                    WARD HILL LAMON (V.O.)
               *We never found the man who loosed
               those bolts, but we did uncover a
               most heinous plan.*

                    WARD HILL LAMON (V.O.)
               *Seeking to kill Mr. Lincoln by
               infecting him with yellow fever...*

        On the bed lies a shipping trunk.

                    WARD HILL LAMON (V.O.)
               *...they gathered clothing from
               victims of the disease in Bermuda.*

        The trunk is labelled, "A. Lincoln, Executive Mansion."

                    WARD HILL LAMON (V.O.)
               *Our detective work saved Mr. Lincoln,
               but I never could be at ease while
               absent from his side.*

90   INT. LINCOLN'S OFFICE - NIGHT   90

        Lamon makes coffee with a Victorian era balance-siphon.
        Lincoln drips wax on a letter.

                    WARD HILL LAMON
                  (to Lincoln)
               I am asked to be Master of Ceremonies
               at the dedication of the cemetery in
               Gettysburg. It is a great honor...

        Lincoln seals the letter.

                    WARD HILL LAMON (CONT'D)
               ...but as I cannot leave your side,
               I will tender my regrets. Of
               course, you could come and deliver
               a few appropriate remarks, but at
               such a time as this, for you to
               leave the Capital... It is not
               possible and I would not presume-

                    LINCOLN
               I will come.

This is the only photograph of President Lincoln at Gettysburg. He is the hatless man center left. The towering figure in the black hat standing nearby is faithful friend and bodyguard, Ward Hill Lamon. Lamon was Marshal of Ceremonies that day, and he introduced President Lincoln at the Gettysburg Address.

Lincoln's Gettysburg Address, Gettysburg, PA, November 19, 1863
Film negative, Library of Congress.

Lamon's look: "You will?"

Lincoln nods. Lamon hands him a cup of coffee. They drink.

91   EXT. CEMETERY HILL - DAY   91

Lamon wears the Marshal of Ceremonies sash. He sits beside
Lincoln and other DIGNITARIES on a platform.

SUPER: GETTYSBURG, PA - NOVEMBER 19, 1863

Lamon rises, takes a step forward, and bellows:

                    WARD HILL LAMON
          THE PRESIDENT OF THE UNITED STATES!

Lamon sits. Lincoln stands. Takes a long look over the crowd.

                    WARD HILL LAMON (V.O.)
          Resistance to the war was growing.
          The draft riots in New York caused
          more deaths than many battles. Mr.
          Lincoln needed to reinvigorate the
          people. To explain to them - and
          perhaps himself - why this endless
          plague of war must continue.

                    LINCOLN
          Four score and seven years ago our
          fathers brought forth upon this
          continent, a new nation, conceived
          in liberty, and dedicated to the
          proposition that all men are
          created equal.

Faces in the crowd reveal a cross section of America.

                    LINCOLN (CONT'D)
          Now we are engaged in a great civil
          war, testing whether that nation,
          or any nation so conceived and so
          dedicated, can long endure.

A grim but determined WIDOW holding a picture of her husband.

                    LINCOLN (CONT'D)
          We are met on a great battlefield
          of that war. We have come to
          dedicate a portion of that field,
          as a final resting place for those
          who here gave their lives that that
          nation might live.

An African-American GRAVE-DIGGER.

So many boys perished, and we believe President Lincoln felt the loss of every one.

Soldiers' Cemetery, Alexandria, VA, 1865
Glass plate negative, wet collodion, Library of Congress.

                    LINCOLN (CONT'D)
          It is altogether fitting and proper
          that we should do this. But in a
          larger sense, we cannot dedicate -
          we cannot consecrate - we cannot
          hallow this ground.

Three battle-tried PRIVATES.

                    LINCOLN (CONT'D)
          The brave men, living and dead, who
          struggled here, have consecrated it
          far above our power to add or
          detract.

A leathery OLD VETERAN.

                    LINCOLN (CONT'D)
          The world will little note, nor
          long remember what we say here, but
          it can never forget what they did
          here.

PARENTS of a dead soldier holding his picture.

                    LINCOLN (CONT'D)
          It is for us, the living, rather to
          be dedicated here to the unfinished
          work which they who fought here
          have thus far so nobly advanced.

A wizened PREACHER.

                    LINCOLN (CONT'D)
          It is rather for us to be here
          dedicated to the great task
          remaining before us, that from
          these honored dead we take
          increased devotion to that cause
          for which they here gave the last
          full measure of devotion...

A MOTHER and CHILDREN (2).

                    LINCOLN (CONT'D)
          ...that we here highly resolve that
          these dead shall not have died in
          vain; that this nation, under God,
          shall have a new birth of freedom,
          and that government of the people,
          by the people, for the people shall
          not perish from the earth.

Lincoln lets the final words ring and waits. No applause.

The principal orator at the Gettysburg Cemetery Dedication was Edward Everett, former U.S. Senator, Governor of Massachusetts and President of Harvard. He spoke for two hours, and his speech was well received. While it was understood that the President's remarks would be shorter, Lincoln's two minute speech caught most by surprise. According to historian Shelby Foote, the applause for the Gettysburg Address was delayed, scattered, and "barely polite."

Edward Everett
Photographic print, Library of Congress.

                          CROWD
          Is that it? Can't be... It's far
          too short. Can't be over yet....

Lamon APPLAUDS, and others join him, but they can't compete
with the growing ROAR of anger.

92   INT. LINCOLN'S OFFICE - DAY   92

Lincoln looks out the window. Senator Sumner stands behind
him.

                     SEN. CHARLES SUMNER
                  (reading from a newspaper)
          "Silly, flat and dish-watery
          utterances of a man who must be
          pointed out to intelligent
          foreigners as the President."

                          LINCOLN
          I have not had much time for foreign
          policy.

                     SEN. CHARLES SUMNER
          You have lost your own people, sir!
          Three years of slaughter, and no
          end in sight!

Lincoln nods.

                     SEN. CHARLES SUMNER (CONT'D)
          Salmon P. Chase offers your ideals
          without your record. Pomeroy and
          his gang have circulated a letter
          demanding Chase's nomination.

92A   EXT. WHITE HOUSE SOUTH LAWN - DAY - CONTINUOUS   92A

LINCOLN'S POV: Treasurer Chase gets clapped on the back by
congratulatory POLITICIANS.

92B   INT. LINCOLN'S OFFICE - DAY - CONTINUOUS   92B

Sumner walks up close to Lincoln.

                     SEN. CHARLES SUMNER
          Mr. President, McClellan has agreed
          to run for the Democrats. He will
          offer peace with slavery, and the
          people will take it. Unless our
          candidate is Chase. Mr. Lincoln.

Lincoln turns. Sumner's shaky hand reaches out and pulls the
President's fingers toward his own head.

Charles Sumner was attacked on the floor of the U.S. Senate on May 22, 1856 by U.S. Representative Preston Brooks of South Carolina. Brooks beat Sumner with a gold-headed cane until the cane broke. Sumner was blinded by his own blood and collapsed unconscious. He suffered traumatic brain injury, post-traumatic stress disorder, and chronic debilitating pain for the rest of his life. Citizens of the South sent Brooks a slew of replacement, gold-headed canes.

                    SEN. CHARLES SUMNER (CONT'D)
          That is the spot where the blow
          first fell, when I was savagely
          attacked on the floor of the U.S.
          Senate. The perpetrator's cane fell
          down on me 23 times more, because I
          had demanded abolition in Kansas
          when all of my colleagues offered
          compromise. I lay broken for three
          years, unable to resume public
          life, my presidential hopes
          destroyed. Even now, my trembling
          hand betrays me. But I would make
          that speech again, sir, because my
          person is not as important as our
          great mission.

Sumner picks up his hat and coat.

                    SEN. CHARLES SUMNER (CONT'D)
          It is time now for Moses to hand
          the staff to Joshua, so that he may
          lead our people into the promised
          land. Do not fail us, sir.

Sumner exits, his footsteps echoing in the cavernous room.

93   EXT. WHITE HOUSE - NIGHT   93

Lincoln's voice echoes through the building.

                    LINCOLN
          Hill!

94   INT. LINCOLN'S OFFICE - NIGHT   94

Lamon enters, banjo in hand.

                    WARD HILL LAMON
          Coffee or banjo?

                    LINCOLN
          You have heard of the Pomeroy
          circular?

                    WARD HILL LAMON
          I have intercepted a copy.

                    LINCOLN
          Bless you, Hill. Please hand it
          over quietly to the press.

                    WARD HILL LAMON
          But...it exfluncticates you.

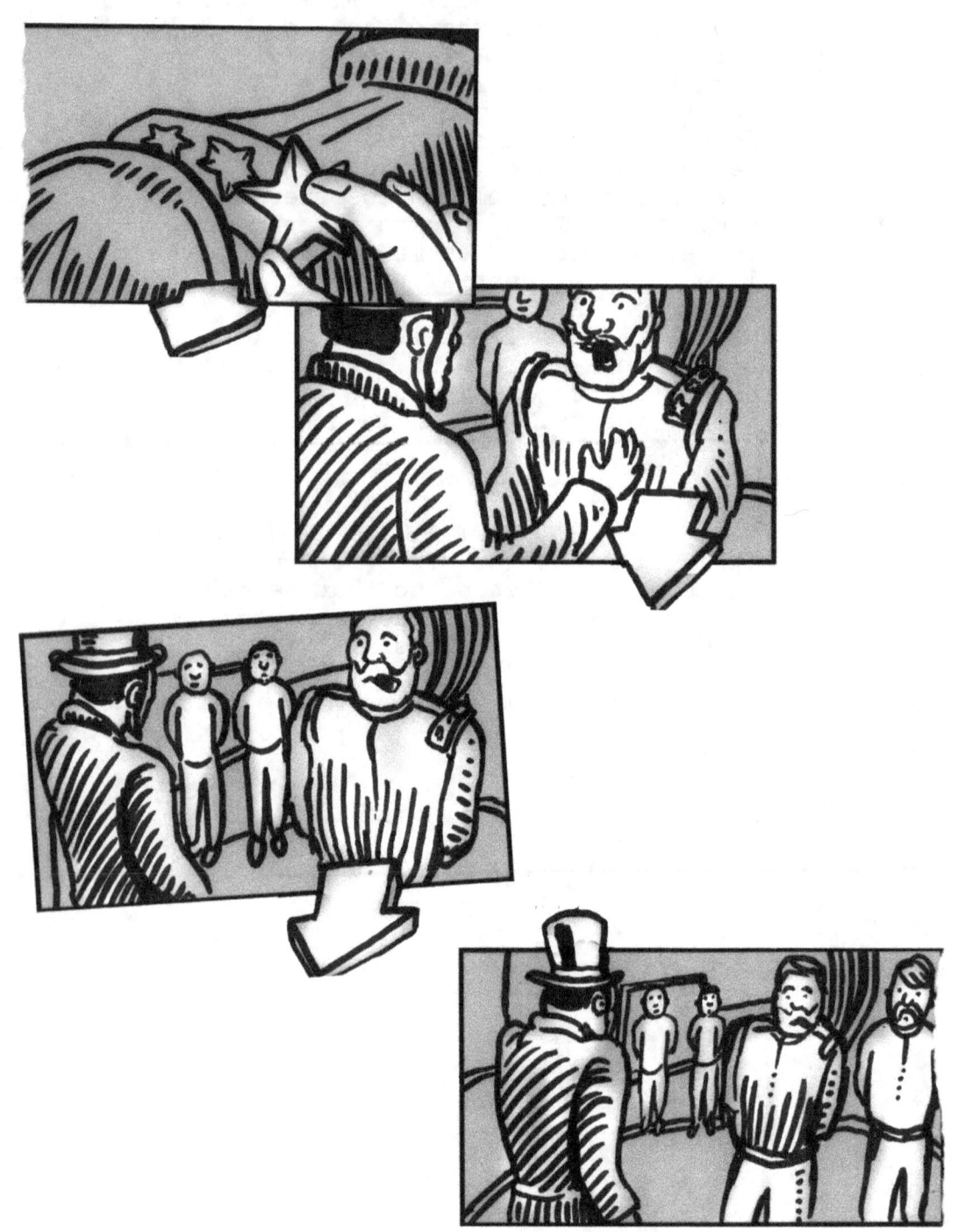

Scene 95 Storyboard - INT. WHITE HOUSE PARLOUR - DAY
Lincoln hands Grant his commission. Pull back to reveal a portrait
of George Washington presiding over the General's promotion.

                    LINCOLN
          If the Almighty wants another man to
          finish my work, one who campaigns for
          my office while serving in my Cabinet,
          who are we to defy him?

                    WARD HILL LAMON
          Ahhhhh. What kills the skunk is the
          publicity it gives itself.

                    LINCOLN
          Aye. And now I shall do what I
          should've done long ago.

95   INT. WHITE HOUSE PARLOUR - DAY   95

     ULYSSES S. GRANT, 41, bearded and stoic, stands erect as
     Lincoln hands him a sealed commission. Sec. of War Stanton,
     Sec. of State Seward, and Lamon look on.

                    LINCOLN
          General Grant, I now promote you to a
          rank last held by General George
          Washington.

                    GENERAL GRANT
          Much obliged, sir, but it won't be
          paper wins this war.

                    LINCOLN
          Tell me your plan.

                    GENERAL GRANT
          I'll run the Eastern armies,
          Sherman the West. We'll hit 'em
          everywhere at once.

                    LINCOLN
          Those not skinning can hold a leg.

                    GENERAL GRANT
          Yes, sir.

     Grant steps closer to Lincoln.

                    GENERAL GRANT (CONT'D)
          Mr President. Win or lose, we keep
          hitting.

                    LINCOLN
          Godspeed.

     Stanton and Seward shake their heads.

                              64.

The Civil War was the first photographed war.

"Mr. Brady has done something to bring home to us the terrible reality and earnestness of war. If he has not brought bodies and laid them in our dooryards and along the streets, he has done something very like it."

- The New York Times
October 20, 1862

Zouave ambulance crew demonstrates removal of wounded soldiers from the battlefield, between 1860 and 1865. Glass plate negative, wet collodion, Library of Congress.

96   INT. TELEGRAPH OFFICE - DAY   96

          Lincoln stands over Major Eckert.

                         MAJOR ECKERT
                    From General Grant: 14,000
                    casualties. He will attack again in
                    the morning.

96A   INT. TELEGRAPH OFFICE - DAY   96A

          Lincoln walks into frame, his back to CAMERA.

                         MAJOR ECKERT
                    17,000 more.

                         LINCOLN
                    My God, 31,000 boys. I cannot bear
                    it. I cannot bear it!

          He walks into CU, stunned.

                         LINCOLN (CONT'D)
                    And yet he advances.

96B   INT. TELEGRAPH OFFICE - DAY   96B

          Lincoln in the same CU looks haggard and unkempt.

                         SEC. OF WAR STANTON
                       (brandishing a dispatch)
                    Another 12,000 at Cold Harbor! Of
                    which 7,000 fell in the first 8
                    minutes!

          Lincoln closes his eyes for a long beat.

                         SEC. OF WAR STANTON (CONT'D)
                    The total is now 54,000, sir! 54,000
                    soldiers in one month!

                         LINCOLN
                       (dazed and forlorn)
                    Thank God for our brave Negro
                    troops. Lee will run out of men
                    before we do.

                         SEC. OF WAR STANTON
                    Mr. President, he must be stopped!

                         LINCOLN
                    Lee will be stopped.

The "photographer's studio" depicted in this plate is actually the Grand Corridor of the White House. It was a perfect fit for the scene due to its overwhelming white light, which is in keeping with the setup of photo studios of the period, as well as thematically apt for *Saving Lincoln*, where we use bright white light to suggest death and destiny.

Grand corridor wing of the White House, Washington, D.C., 1902
Photographic print, Library of Congress.

                    SEC. OF WAR STANTON
          Grant, sir!

                    LINCOLN
          Grant? Grant cannot be stopped.

INT. PHOTOGRAPHY STUDIO - DAY

CLOSE-UP of Lincoln. His eyes look distant and haunted. The
creases in his skin have visibly deepened.

                    PHOTOGRAPHER (O.S.)
          ...3,4,5,6...

Lincoln poses in a sunlit studio.

                    PHOTOGRAPHER (CONT'D)
          ...7,8,9,10.

The Photographer replaces the lens caps on his stereoscopic
camera, then pulls the plate holder off the back.

                    PHOTOGRAPHER (CONT'D)
          Thank you, Mr. President. If you
          could wait a few minutes while I
          develop the plate?

Lincoln nods.

                    TAD (O.S.)
          Let me see them, Hill!

Nearby, Tad and Lamon hold stereoscopes, (small Viewmaster-
like devices used for viewing 3D pictures.) Hundreds of
stereoscopic cards sit on the Photographer's shelves, but Tad
wants the stack in Lamon's hand.

                    WARD HILL LAMON
          These are not for you, Tad. Here,
          look at General Grant on his horse.

                    TAD
          I ain't no Nancy-boy!

Lincoln walks over and hands Tad a photo album.

                    LINCOLN
          Tad, look in here. Tom Thumb, P.T.
          Barnum, Chang and Eng...

The album distracts Tad. Lincoln picks up a stereoscope and
reaches for the stack in Lamon's hand.

                              66.

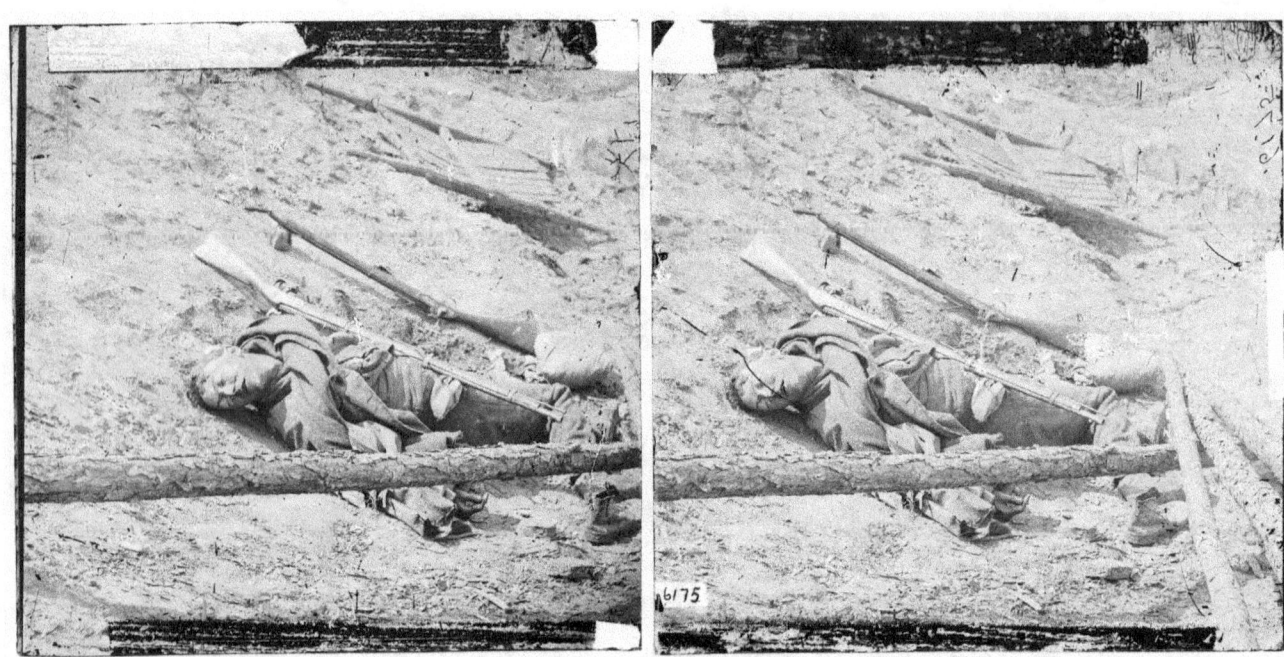

To simulate the experience of looking in a stereoscopic viewer, we chose actual stereographic plates from the Civil war, depicting powerful and haunting images of the fallen. It was very important to the *Saving Lincoln* team that these photos be treated with utmost respect.

Dead Confederate soldier with gun, Petersburg, VA, 1865
Glass plate negative, stereograph, wet collodion, Library of Congress.

                    WARD HILL LAMON
          These are morbid, suh. But look at
          the parrot gun Grant's using at
          Petersburg - 13 inches.

Lincoln takes one of the "morbid" cards and inserts it into
his viewer.

LINCOLN'S POV: highly detailed view of a DEAD BOY,
disemboweled at Gettysburg (an authentic picture.)

He picks up another, and another:

- DEAD BOYS, their abdomens swelling from the heat

- DEAD BOYS, lying in a row before mass burial

- DEAD BOYS, sprawled where they fell by an old fence

- DEAD BOYS in a pile, yards from a whitewashed church

                         TAD
               Pa, can I see?

Lincoln puts down the viewer and hugs his son tightly.

                    TAD (CONT'D)
               Can't I see it, Pa?

                       LINCOLN
               Hill, take him home.

                    WARD HILL LAMON
               I'd prefer to stay with...

Lincoln's look: "Do it."

               WARD HILL LAMON (CONT'D)
          Come, Tad, we'll get a lemon ice.

                         TAD
               Can I get strawberry?

                    WARD HILL LAMON
               My favorite.

                         TAD
          Three cheers for Hill! Hip hip...

Lamon and Tad exit. Lincoln continues viewing:

- DEAD BOY, thrown on a rock

- DEAD BOY, lying on his rifle

Nettie Colburn was a young medium who channeled "spirits" in an effort to help people communicate with the departed. The Spiritualism movement gained popularity during the Civil War because so many people lost loved ones. Whether a fraud or not - and she was never proven to be one - Nettie Colburn provided great comfort to Mary Todd Lincoln. (Image from her book - see next page)

- DEAD BOY, decaying

Lincoln keeps looking at the gruesome images.

98   INT. WHITE HOUSE VESTIBULE - NIGHT   98

Lincoln enters, his face grim. Mary, still dressed in
elaborate mourning clothes, is waiting for him.

                    MARY
          There you are! Have you forgotten
          your promise? Nettie Colburn is
          here! Everyone's waiting.

99   INT. WHITE HOUSE PARLOUR - NIGHT   99

NETTIE COLBURN, 19, delicate, wide-eyed, and sincere,
curtsies before the President.

                    MARY
          My I present, Nettie Colburn.

                    LINCOLN
          So this is the famous Nettie.

                    NETTIE COLBURN
          Yes, sir. So honored, sir. I insisted
          my father vote for you...

She speaks like a school girl. Also present are Mary, Mrs.
Keckly, Lamon, and CRANSTON LAURIE, 60's, an old fashioned
gentleman.

                    CRANSTON LAURIE
          Mr. President, an honor, sir.

Lincoln nods.

                    CRANSTON LAURIE (CONT'D)
          We are accustomed to sit in a
          circle and join hands, sir, though
          it is not strictly necessary.

Lincoln does not extend his hands. He sits on a chair facing
Nettie, who sits on an ottoman. Others sit nearby.

Mary grasps Mrs. Keckly's hand. Nettie Colburn's head begins
to sway.

                    CRANSTON LAURIE (CONT'D)
          We wait until one of our spirit
          friends takes control of Miss
          Colburn.

68.

"Those present declared that they lost sight of the timid girl in the majesty of the utterance, the strength and force of the language and the importance of that which was conveyed, and seemed to realize that some strong masculine spirit force was giving speech to almost divine commands."

- Nettie Colburn Maynard, from her book,
  *Was Abraham Lincoln a Spiritualist? or, Curious
  Revelations from the Life of a Trance Medium*

                    NETTIE COLBURN
            (husky voice, country accent)
        Mr. President, pleased to make your
        acquaintance. Ezra Bamford, M.D.

Nettie extends her hand like a man and shakes with Lincoln.

                    WARD HILL LAMON
        Now I've seen the elephant.

                    MARY
        Shhh!

                    NETTIE COLBURN/DR. BAMFORD
            (to Lincoln)
        Sir, I have traveled a long way to
        tell you this: stand fast by General
        Grant, and Richmond will be yours.

                    LINCOLN
        Are you a military doctor then?

                    NETTIE COLBURN/DR. BAMFORD
        No, I was a country doctor. But I
        am given to know that strong
        parties urge you to dismiss Grant.
        They say the cost is too high,
        he'll never prevail, he'll cost you
        the election. But, Mr. President,
        you must in no wise heed such coun-
        sel. Stand firm behind your
        convictions and fearlessly perform
        the work for which you have been
        elevated.

                    LINCOLN
        This you are "given to know?"

                    NETTIE COLBURN/DR. BAMFORD
        I am, sir.

                    LINCOLN
        And are you given to know how many
        boys have crossed into your realm
        thanks to the work I have already
        performed?

                    NETTIE COLBURN/DR. BAMFORD
        A great many.

                    LINCOLN
        300,000, Dr. Bamford. An entire
        city of boys.

We added columns of smoke from the Battle of Fort Stevens to this striking cityscape, and used it as a facsimile for Washington City.

Nashville, TN. View from Capitol, 1864
Glass plate negative, wet collodion, Library of Congress.

                    NETTIE COLBURN/DR. BAMFORD
          They made the sacrifice proudly.

                    LINCOLN
          You dare speak for them? Do you speak
          for their mothers as well?!

                    NETTIE COLBURN/DR. BAMFORD
          Yours is not an easy task, Mr.
          President. You bear it heroically.

                    LINCOLN
          Heroically?! I condemn multitudes
          with a pen! I am incompetent! And
          it was my own self-serving ambition
          which elevated me!

Lincoln stands and exits, SLAMMING the door behind him.

100   EXT. WASHINGTON D.C. - DAY   100

Panoramic view of Washington looking north from the White
House. Sound of distant ARTILLERY. Faraway smoke.

                    WARD HILL LAMON (V.O.)
          General Grant's war of attrition
          finally began to work. Hoping to
          buy time, and seize much needed
          supplies, the enemy launched an
          attack upon Washington City itself.

101   EXT. FORT STEVENS - DAY   101

Lincoln strides toward the fort, with Lamon at his elbow.

SUPER: JULY 12, 1864

                    WARD HILL LAMON
          No President has ever stood on the
          field of battle!

Lincoln keeps walking.

                    WARD HILL LAMON (CONT'D)
          Your place, suh, is on that boat!

Lincoln approaches the entrance.

                    WARD HILL LAMON (CONT'D)
                    (blocking Lincoln)
          Must Mary bury another Lincoln?!

These distinctive fortifications are known as an "abatis."

Point of Rocks, VA. Redoubt "Zabriskie."
Glass plate negative, wet collodion, Library of Congress.

Legend has it that the Union Captain who told Lincoln to "Get down!" was Oliver Wendell Holmes, Jr. (1840 -1935). Photo from Wikimedia Commons.

                         LINCOLN
              Lieutenant, remove Marshal Lamon
              from the fort!

TWO SOLDIERS grab Lamon and pull him away.

                       WARD HILL LAMON
              Lincoln!

Struggling mightily, Lamon manages to throw off one soldier.

Lincoln gets closer to the parapet.

Lamon throws off the other soldier, but an OFFICER puts a gun
to his head.

                         OFFICER
                      (to Soldiers)
              You! You! Seize him!

They drag Lamon off.

Meanwhile, Lincoln climbs the parapet. As he approaches the
wall, an ARTILLERY MAN behind him is hit - blood everywhere.

SLO-MO/LINCOLN'S POV: The battlefield comes into view.
CONFEDERATE SOLDIERS fire in his direction.

SLO-MO: Lincoln stares out at the battle. Behind him, a UNION
SURGEON runs over to help the Artillery Man.

SLO-MO: A UNION CAPTAIN sees Lincoln.

                       UNION CAPTAIN
                       (distorted)
              You there, get down!

SLO-MO: a REBEL SHARPSHOOTER notices Lincoln on the parapet
and points him out to a SECOND SHARPSHOOTER. They both take
careful aim at the President.

SLO-MO: Lincoln closes his eyes.

SLO-MO: The Sharpshooters FIRE.

SLO-MO: Lincoln's eyes open. BULLETS tear the air within
inches of his face.

SLO-MO: The Union Surgeon behind Lincoln is hit.

                  UNION CAPTAIN (CONT'D)
                       (distorted)
              Get that damn fool OFF MY PARAPET!

"It was the havoc of the war, the sacrifice of patriotic lives, the flow of human blood, the mangling of precious limbs in the great Union host that shocked him most, indeed on some occasions shocked him almost beyond his capacity to control either his judgment or his feelings."

- Ward Hill Lamon, *Recollections of Abraham Lincoln*

SLO-MO: Lincoln keeps staring out at the field. Two UNION
GUNNERS appear behind him and pull him off the parapet.

RESUME NORMAL SPEED: Lincoln stumbles down the ramp and falls
on the ground. He rises, and starts back up the ramp, but...

Lamon rushes in, grabs Lincoln, and shoves him into a
sheltered nook between the ramp and parapet.

                    WARD HILL LAMON
          Lincoln, you will stop!

                    LINCOLN
          Release me!

                    WARD HILL LAMON
          I shall not! For three years I have
          fought spies, traitors, and assassins
          who seek to destroy you. And yet more
          than any of them, it is you - you,
          suh - who endangers the life of the
          only man fit to command our ship of
          state!

                    LINCOLN
               (struggling to break free)
          Lieutenant!

                    WARD HILL LAMON
          BE STILL!

Lamon's furious eyes bore into Lincoln's. CANNON ROARS!

                    WARD HILL LAMON (CONT'D)
          You answer me one question, and
          then you may return to the cannon's
          mouth, and the devil take you!

                    LINCOLN
          ...Well?!

                    WARD HILL LAMON
          When you stood in the line of fire,
          other men fell. Why was your life
          spared?

                    LINCOLN
          ...I don't know.

                    WARD HILL LAMON
          Because, suh, you are Commander-in-
          Chief of an army fighting a
          necessary war.

Frame from *Saving Lincoln*. Lamon worked endless hours protecting Lincoln, but Lincoln worked even longer hours protecting the nation.

CANNON ROARS nearby.

>   WARD HILL LAMON (CONT'D)
>   And that army must take life! I
>   know you hate it. It is a terrible
>   destiny, suh, but if you did not
>   hate it so, the Almighty Himself
>   would not have selected you for it!

CANNON ROARS overhead. Lamon flinches, but Lincoln remains
steady, still taking it all in.

>   LINCOLN
>   Hill, I...

>   WARD HILL LAMON
>   ...yes?

>   LINCOLN
>   I must return to the White House.

Lamon nearly collapses in exhausted relief.

>   WARD HILL LAMON
>   (to God)
>   Thank you!

>   LINCOLN
>   (grasping Lamon's arms)
>   Thank you, Hill.

>   WARD HILL LAMON
>   Well... 'at's why you brung me.
>   Now, come!

CANNON ROARS. Lamon pulls Lincoln up and, sheltering him from
flying debris, leads him out of the fort.

104   INT. LINCOLN'S OFFICE - NIGHT   104

Lincoln works on a document beneath a dim light. Lamon sleeps
on the couch.

>   WARD HILL LAMON (V.O.)
>   *Mr. Lincoln's melancholy retreated,*
>   *but my little speech at Fort*
>   *Stevens also produced a perilous*
>   *back fire...*

Lincoln puts down his pen, lays a blanket over Lamon and
exits.

The North Portico of the White House was lit by gas sconces from 1852 until 1902, when the famous electric lantern pictured to the left was installed. We removed it for Scene 106.

106   EXT. WHITE HOUSE PORTICO - DAY   106

Early morning. Lincoln arrives at the mansion. Lamon stands
on the steps, scowling.

                    LINCOLN
          I have something to tell you!

Lincoln pulls Lamon inside.

107   INT. WHITE HOUSE EAST ROOM - DAY   107

Lincoln leads Lamon into the deserted East Room.

                    LINCOLN
          You know how I hate to ride about
          with armed guards.

                    WARD HILL LAMON
          I have observed the phenomenon.

                    LINCOLN
          Well, you needn't worry any longer.

                    WARD HILL LAMON
          Much obliged! Just wake me up
          before you absquatulate into the
          night.

                    LINCOLN
          I mean, the guards will no longer
          be necessary.

                    WARD HILL LAMON
          Come again?

                    LINCOLN
          Hill, last night I rode out to the
          Summer Residence alone.

                    WARD HILL LAMON
          I know!

                    LINCOLN
          I was jogging along at a slow gait,
          immersed in contemplation,
          suddenly... BANG! I was separated
          from my eight-dollar plug hat, with
          no assent on my part express or
          implied. It was returned to me this
          morning - rather the worse for
          wear, I'm afraid.

The East Room of the White House in *Saving Lincoln* bears some 20th century influences, but we chose to use this image because it offers high resolution and multiple coverage angles.

White House, East Room, between 1905 and 1945
Glass plate negative, Library of Congress.

Lincoln hands Lamon the hat. Holding it up to the light,
Lamon looks through a <u>bullet-hole</u> in the crown.

> WARD HILL LAMON
> This is your evidence for the
> claim, "I need no guards?!"

> LINCOLN
> Hill, the Almighty spared me for a
> purpose.

> WARD HILL LAMON
> Yes, He did, but it would be a sin
> to rely on His good nature when you
> have earthly guards close at hand!

> LINCOLN
> Hill, I see it now. I will be
> spared until my purpose is
> accomplished.

> WARD HILL LAMON
> But-

> LINCOLN
> And then, when the war is finally
> won, I shall be gathered unto
> Willie, Ellsworth, Ned, and all the
> other boys - the veil between them
> and me is thin already. But I will
> not be taken until then. This hat
> is the proof.

Lamon GROANS in utter frustration.

> WARD HILL LAMON
> Lincoln, what if last night was
> simply a near miss? And you are
> alive today because I have
> repeatedly saved you these past four
> years?

> LINCOLN
> Why, then, my friend, we are both
> God's instruments.

A sharp KNOCK, a door opens, and Hay bursts in.

> HAY
> Mr. President! The Secretary of
> War!

Stanton marches in waving a telegraphic dispatch.

White House Corridor, between 1905 and 1945
Glass plate negative Library of Congress.

"While I am deeply sensible to the high compliment of a re-election; and duly grateful, as I trust, to Almighty God for having directed my countrymen to a right conclusion, as I think, for their own good, it adds nothing to my satisfaction that any other man may be disappointed or pained by the result."

- Abraham Lincoln, November 10, 1864

                    SEC. OF WAR STANTON
          Message from Sherman.
               (reading)
          "Atlanta is ours and fairly won."

Lincoln looks stunned. Hay and Stanton grin broadly. Lamon's
features soften.

                    LINCOLN
          YIPPEE!

110   INT. WHITE HOUSE UPSTAIRS CORRIDOR - NIGHT   110

Lincoln exchanges happy good-nights with Stanton, Seward, and
other members of the inner circle, as they depart.

                    WARD HILL LAMON (V.O.)
          The fall of Atlanta transformed the
          national mood. Candidate McClellan
          was all but forgotten, and Mr.
          Lincoln swept to a second term.

                    SEC. OF STATE SEWARD
          Four more years, Mr. President! The
          war nearly won! Think of what we
          can achieve! Think Alaska.

                    LINCOLN
               (laughing)
          Let the war be won, Mr. Seward,
          we'll explore that possibility.

Finally, only Lamon is left, and Lincoln regards him warmly.

                    WARD HILL LAMON
          I have given the matter much
          thought. I now release you from
          your promise.

                    LINCOLN
          My promise?

                    WARD HILL LAMON
          I will sacrifice my Ambassadorship
          to France so that you may retain my
          companionship here.

                    LINCOLN
          I see. Ward Hill Lamon, you have
          the thanks of a grateful nation,
          and my own. Good night, old friend.

Lamon exits. Lincoln enters his bedroom and shuts the door.

General William Tecumseh Sherman was superintendent of the Louisiana State Military Academy before the war. He knew the Southern mind and was the first to warn Lincoln that the war would be long and brutal. In 1864, Sherman led his men on a 300 mile march from Atlanta to the sea.

"We cannot change the hearts and minds of those people of the South, but we can make war so terrible...that generations would pass away before they would again appeal to it."

- William Tecumseh Sherman

General William Tecumseh Sherman, 1865, Wikimedia Commons.

Lamon returns. He removes his coat, sits on the floor in front of the President's bedroom, and lays out his arsenal of pistols and bowie knives.

Then, he pulls out his whiskey flask, takes a swig, covers himself with his coat, and falls asleep.

111   INT. TELEGRAPH OFFICE - DAY   111

Lincoln and Stanton study the joined maps of the Eastern and Western theaters of war.

                    WARD HILL LAMON (V.O.)
          *Sherman now planned a thousand-mile
          march through the heart of the
          South in order to join Grant at
          Richmond.*

Lincoln nods, "Yes." Stanton signals Major Eckert, who immediately starts telegraphing.

                    WARD HILL LAMON (V.O.)
          *Sherman made Georgia howl. But as
          the rebels were cornered, so they
          became more dangerous.*

112   EXT. 7TH STREET PIKE - NIGHT   112

Lamon gallops furiously up the familiar road.

                    WARD HILL LAMON (V.O.)
          *Their next plot was almost
          admirable for its sheer ambition.
          Mr. Lincoln was to be kidnapped and
          exchanged for 200,000 prisoners.*

112A   EXT. SUMMER RESIDENCE - NIGHT   112A

As Lamon rides up to the Summer Residence, THREE MENACING MEN emerge from the darkened house; two carry directional lanterns.

                    WARD HILL LAMON
          Halt and identify yourselves!

They point their lanterns at Lamon, and draw their guns. Though blinded, Lamon draws both of his revolvers.

                    MENACING LEADER
          Throw down your weapons now!

                    WARD HILL LAMON
          I will throw down your souls before
          I throw down my-

"My anxiety about Mr. Lincoln that evening grew out of a report of an alarming character made to me by one of my detectives. Stanton had threatening news also, and was therefore excited about Mr. Lincoln's safety. He told me that he never had so great a scare in his life as he had that night. The brusque Secretary thought the deputy marshal and I were assassins. The incident provoked much merriment among the parties concerned, no one enjoying the serio-comic part of it more than Mr. Lincoln himself."

- Ward Hill Lamon, *Recollections of Abraham Lincoln*

Hon. Edwin Stanton, between 1855 and 1865
Glass plate negative, wet collodion, Library of Congress.

                    MENACING LEADER
          Marshal Lamon, is that you?

                    WARD HILL LAMON
          ...Mr. Stanton?

                    MENACING LEADER/STANTON
          Is the President with you?

                    WARD HILL LAMON
          No, suh, I come in search of him!

                    SEC. OF WAR STANTON
          He is not here, and I am growing
          exceedingly concerned for his
          safety.

                    WARD HILL LAMON
          As am I, suh. As am I...

Lamon rides off.

113   EXT. WHITE HOUSE PORTICO - NIGHT   113

Lincoln descends from a fancy carriage. Senator Sumner and a
FOREIGN MINISTER sit inside.

                    LINCOLN
          Good night, Senator. Good night,
          Your Excellency.

                    CARRIAGE OCCUPANTS
          Good night, Mr. President!

The carriage rolls away, revealing an infuriated Lamon.

                    LINCOLN
          Hill, there you are. Good evening!

                    WARD HILL LAMON
          You went to the theater.

                    LINCOLN
          Oh, yes. Superior *Othello*.

                    WARD HILL LAMON
          You went to the theater unattended.

                    LINCOLN
          No, I-

"Mr. Lincoln had in his great heart no place for uncharitableness or suspicion; which accounts for his singular indifference to the numberless cautions so earnestly and persistently pressed upon him by friends who knew the danger to which he was hourly exposed. He had a sublime faith in human nature; and in that faith he lived until the fatal moment when the nations of the earth were startled by a tragedy whose mournful consequences no man can measure."

- Ward Hill Lamon, *Recollections of Abraham Lincoln*

William Herndon, ca. 1875, Wikimedia Commons.

                    WARD HILL LAMON
        When I say unattended, I mean you
        went with Charles Sumner and a
        foreign minister, neither of whom
        could defend himself against the
        assault of an able-bodied woman!

Lincoln nods in reluctant agreement.

                    WARD HILL LAMON (CONT'D)
        You know that your life is sought
        after, and that I have provided men
        to safeguard your person. I myself
        am always ready to perform the duty,
        when I am not out playing the
        detective. Yet, despite all of this,
        you choose to elude us. So be it.
        But I will not pass into history as
        the man who lost Lincoln. You shall
        have my resignation in the morning.

                    LINCOLN
        I... cannot fault you.

Lamon gets too choked up to respond. Lincoln regards his
friend with infinite compassion.

Lamon grabs Lincoln and hugs him.

                    WARD HILL LAMON
        I shall miss you, suh.

Then Lamon pushes Lincoln away and jumps on his horse, looks
back once, and rides into the night.

114   INT. ILLINOIS STATEHOUSE - NIGHT - **FLASH FORWARD**   114

                    BILLY HERNDON
        Perhaps Mr. Lincoln did not fault
        you but I do!

                    WARD HILL LAMON
        There is more.

                    BILLY HERNDON
        I have heard enough!

Over Lincoln's coffin, Billy Herndon pulls his <u>cane dagger</u>
and points it at Lamon.

                    LEONARD SWETT
        Let him finish, Billy.

When Sherman began his march to the sea, he lost communication with Washington. Many feared his army might be vulnerable in such hostile territory.

" I know the hole he went in at, but I can't tell you what hole he will come out of."

- Abraham Lincoln, December, 1864

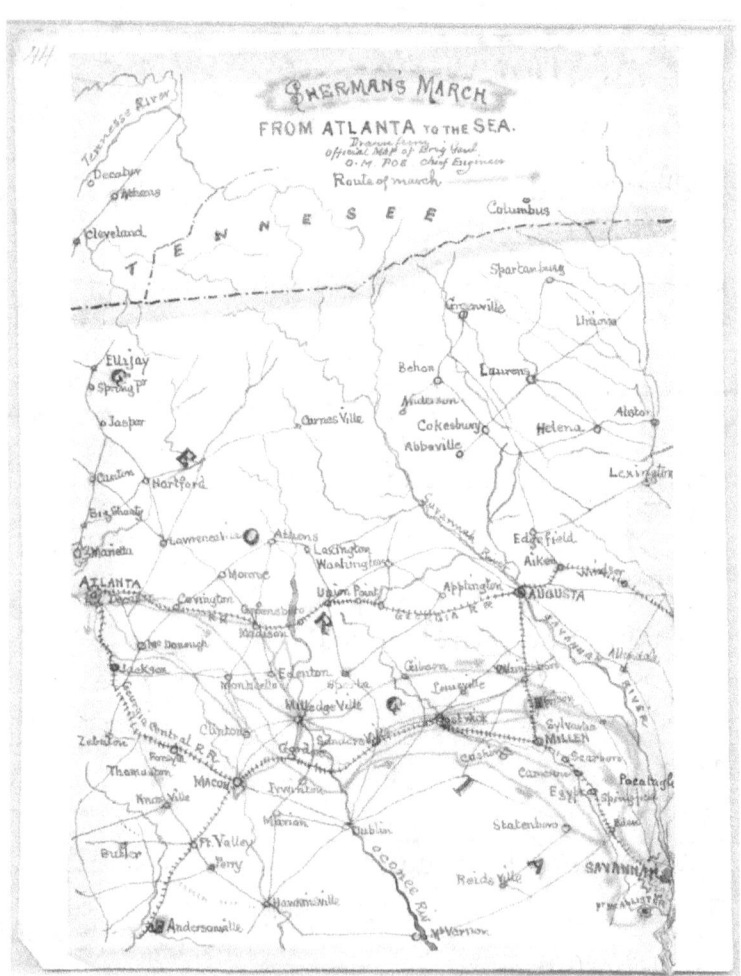

Sherman's march from Atlanta to the sea. Drawn from official map of Brig. Genl. O. M. Poe, Chief Engineer, 1861 to 1865, Library of Congress.

We see a large Christmas tree. Mary, still in mourning, and
Mrs. Keckly wrap cakes in wax paper, then add them to a crate
labelled "Freedmen's Relief Fund."

Lincoln sips tea with Sec. of State Seward and Sen. Sumner.

> LINCOLN
> My wife is as handsome as when she
> was a girl, and I, a poor nobody,
> fell in love with her. And what is
> more, I have never fallen out.

Mary pretends not to hear, but she exchanges a little smile
with Mrs. Keckly as she turns to wrap another cake.

Sec. of War Stanton enters.

> SEC. OF WAR STANTON
> The lost army is found.

> SEC. OF STATE SEWARD
> News from Sherman!

Stanton carries two documents. He hands one to Lincoln.

> LINCOLN
> (reading)
> "Mr. President, I beg to present to
> you as a Christmas gift, the city of
> Savannah."

> SEC. OF STATE SEWARD
> Marvelous tidings!

> SEN. CHARLES SUMNER
> Now he has only to transect the
> Carolinas and...

> SEC. OF WAR STANTON
> Mr. President, a word if you please.

Stanton speaks with Lincoln in hushed tones.

> SEC. OF WAR STANTON
> Where is Lamon?

> LINCOLN
> He was called away.

The following ad was run in the Selma Dispatch by George W. Gayle, a lawyer from Cahaba, Alabama:

One Million Dollars Wanted, to have Peace by the 1st of March. – If the citizens of the Southern Confederacy will furnish me with the cash or good securities for the sum of one million dollars, I will cause the lives of Abraham Lincoln, William H. Seward and Andrew Johnson to be taken by the first of March next. This will give us peace, and satisfy the world that cruel tyrants can not live in the "land of liberty." If this is not accomplished nothing will be claimed beyond the sum of fifty thousand dollars, in advance, which is supposed to be necessary to reach and slaughter the three villains. I will give, myself, one thousand dollars towards this patriotic purpose. Every one wishing to contribute will address box X, Cahaba, Alabama. December 1, 1864

SEC. OF WAR STANTON
He must be called back. This is an
advertisement now running in the
Southern papers: "If the citizens
of the Confederacy will furnish me
with cash or good securities in the
sum of one million dollars, I will
cause the lives of Abraham Lincoln,
William H. Seward, and Andrew
Johnson to be taken by the first of
March next."

LINCOLN
The Secretary of State will be
honored to be mentioned ahead of
the Vice President.

SEC. OF WAR STANTON
Do you joke, sir?

LINCOLN
Mr. Stanton, that man will never
raise a cold million.

SEC. OF WAR STANTON
He has only to apply in Montreal!
Rebel agents are disbursing enormous
sums there for just such operations.
Killers are coming, sir! It is the
enemy's only hope! And your
continued disregard for the
Presidential person is nigh unto
treason.

LINCOLN
I believe I will be spared, Mr.
Stanton, at least until the war-

SEC. OF WAR STANTON
Just answer - where is Lamon?

LINCOLN
I cannot say.

117   EXT. WHITE HOUSE - NIGHT   117

Two SENTRIES pace the grounds.

Lurking behind a tree, a BLACK-CLAD ASSASSIN watches them.

118   INT. LINCOLN'S OFFICE - NIGHT   118

Lincoln sits at his desk, writing. He stops to review.

"At this second appearing to take the oath of the Presidential office there is less occasion for an extended address than there was at the first. Then a statement somewhat in detail of a course to be pursued seemed fitting and proper. Now, at the expiration of four years, during which public declarations have been constantly called forth on every point and phase of the great contest which still absorbs the attention and engrosses the energies of the nation, little that is new could be presented. The progress of our arms, upon which all else chiefly depends, is as well known to the public as to myself, and it is, I trust, reasonably satisfactory and encouraging to all. With high hope for the future, no prediction in regard to it is ventured.

"On the occasion corresponding to this four years ago all thoughts were anxiously directed to an impending civil war. All dreaded it, all sought to avert it. While the inaugural address was being delivered from this place, devoted altogether to saving the Union without war, insurgent agents were in the city seeking to destroy it without war—seeking to dissolve the Union and divide effects by negotiation. Both parties deprecated war, but one of them would make war rather than let the nation survive, and the other would accept war rather than let it perish, and the war came.

"One-eighth of the whole population were colored slaves, not distributed generally over the Union, but localized in the southern part of it. These slaves constituted a peculiar and powerful interest. All knew that this interest was somehow the cause of the war. To strengthen, perpetuate, and extend this interest was the object for which the insurgents would rend the Union even by war, while the Government claimed no right to do more than to restrict the territorial enlargement of it. Neither party expected for the war the magnitude or the duration which it has already attained. Neither anticipated that the cause of the conflict might cease with or even before the conflict itself should cease. Each looked for an easier triumph, and a result less fundamental and astounding. Both read the same Bible and pray to the same God, and each invokes His aid against the other. It may seem strange that any men should dare to ask a just God's assistance in wringing their bread from the sweat of other men's faces, but let us judge not, that we be not judged. The prayers of both could not be answered. That of neither has been answered fully. The Almighty has His own purposes. 'Woe unto the world because of offenses; for it must needs be that offenses come, but woe to that man by whom the offense cometh.' If we shall suppose that American slavery is one of those offenses which, in the providence of God, must needs come, but which, having continued through His appointed time, He now wills to remove, and that He gives to both North and South this terrible war as the woe due to those by whom the offense came, shall we discern therein any departure from those divine attributes which the believers in a living God always ascribe to Him? Fondly do we hope, fervently do we pray, that this mighty scourge of war may speedily pass away. Yet, if God wills that it continue until all the wealth piled by the bondsman's two hundred and fifty years of unrequited toil shall be sunk, and until every drop of blood drawn with the lash shall be paid by another drawn with the sword, as was said three thousand years ago, so still it must be said 'the judgments of the Lord are true and righteous altogether.'

"With malice toward none, with charity for all, with firmness in the right as God gives us to see the right, let us strive on to finish the work we are in, to bind up the nation's wounds, to care for him who shall have borne the battle and for his widow and his orphan, to do all which may achieve and cherish a just and lasting peace among ourselves and with all nations."

- Abraham Lincoln's Second Inaugural Address

                          LINCOLN
                       (reading)
              "Both read the same Bible and pray
              to the same God. It may seem
              strange..."

119   EXT. WHITE HOUSE - NIGHT   119

The Sentry crosses the driveway. The Assassin darts across
the lawn and disappears behind the White House.

120   INT. LINCOLN'S OFFICE - NIGHT   120

Lincoln dips his pen and writes:

"...that any men should dare to ask..."

121   EXT. WHITE HOUSE - NIGHT   121

Assassin inches along a cornice.

122   INT. LINCOLN'S OFFICE - NIGHT   122

Lincoln writes and reads aloud:

                       LINCOLN (O.S.)
              "...a just God's assistance in
              wringing their bread from the sweat
              of other men's faces..."

123   EXT/INT. WHITE HOUSE/LINCOLN'S OFFICE - NIGHT   123

Inching along a cornice, the Assassin looks into a window.

ASSASSIN'S POV: Lincoln sits at his desk, still writing:

"...but let us judge not, that we be not judged..."

ASSASSIN'S POV: a BODYGUARD is visible in the hall, asleep.

The Assassin nudges Lincoln's window upward.

Lincoln doesn't notice. A crackling fire roars in the
fireplace.

The window rises further. The Assassin pulls out his pistol.

The Assassin jumps into the room. Aims his gun at Lincoln.

                          ASSASSIN
              Bang.

Lincoln jumps up in fright. But the "Assassin" is Lamon.

Scene 124 Storyboard - EXT. CAPITOL BUILDING - DAY
An agitated John Wilkes Booth emerges from the crowd and
approaches camera.

"District of Columbia, County of Washington: Robert Strong, a citizen of
said County and District, being duly sworn says that he was a policeman at
the Capitol on the day of the second inauguration of President Lincoln...
when a man in a very determined and excited manner broke through the
line of policemen which had been formed to keep the crowd out. Lieutenant
Westfall immediately seized the stranger and a considerable scuffle ensued.
The stranger seemed determined to get to the platform... but the intruder
was finally thrust from the passage... After the President was assassinated...
Westfall procured a photograph of the assassin Booth.... The commissioner
examined it attentively and said, "Yes I would know that face among ten
thousand. That is the man you had a scuffle with on inauguration day. That is
the same man." Robert Strong, sworn to and subscribed before me this 20th
day of March 1876 James A Tait, seal Notary Public.

- Affidavit included in Ward Hill Lamon's
Recollections of Abraham Lincoln

                    ASSASSIN/WARD HILL LAMON
          Have you any idea how easy it is to
          reach your person?

                    LINCOLN
          Did you plan to kill me yourself,
          by way of extreme fright?

                    WARD HILL LAMON
          It is the guards around this
          mansion who will soon suffer
          extreme fright.

                    LINCOLN
               (grinning)
          Are you back then?

                    WARD HILL LAMON
          Well, if I am to be the man who
          lost Lincoln, at least I shall do
          so while standing my post.

                    LINCOLN
          Good. I need a proper Marshal of
          Ceremonies.

124   EXT. CAPITOL BUILDING - DAY   124

White skies. Union flags everywhere. CROWDS beginning to
gather.

Lamon, wearing the Marshal of Ceremonies sash, addresses his
Deputies and other GUARDS on the Capitol steps.

                    WARD HILL LAMON
          If any of you should fail to
          protect the President, God have
          mercy on your soul, for I shall
          have none. Take your posts.

The Guards fan out.

SUPER: MARCH 4, 1865

The Crowd swells, growing larger and larger.

A strikingly HANDSOME MAN, 27, elegantly dressed, works his
way toward the Capitol steps.

                    WARD HILL LAMON (V.O.) (CONT'D)
          Everyone knows what throngs assemble
          to witness the inauguration of a
          President of the United States.

Abraham Lincoln delivering his second inaugural address as President of the United States
Washington, D.C., March 4, 1865
Photographic print, albumen silver, Library of Congress.

Abraham Lincoln (standing)

Ward Hill Lamon (top hat & goatee)

CONGRESSMEN, JUSTICES and others fill the VIP platform.

> WARD HILL LAMON (V.O.) (CONT'D)
> *It is astonishing that any man*
> *could have seriously entertained*
> *the thought of assassinating Mr.*
> *Lincoln in the presence of such a*
> *concourse of citizens.*

As the crowd thickens around him, the Handsome Man pushes and shoves toward his goal.

> WARD HILL LAMON (V.O.) (CONT'D)
> *And yet, there was such a man in*
> *the assemblage. He was there for*
> *the single purpose of murdering our*
> *leader, in the vain hope that the*
> *South might thereby rise again.*

The BAND plays "Hail to the Chief." Lincoln emerges on the portico.

The Handsome Man breaks though to the front of the crowd, where Lamon's Guards form a wall.

> WARD HILL LAMON (V.O.) (CONT'D)
> *That man was John Wilkes Booth.*

Lincoln approaches, shaking hands with dozens of VIP's.

The Handsome Man/Booth (last seen in heavy theatrical makeup) tries to shove past Lamon's Guards. A scuffle ensues.

> JOHN WILKES BOOTH
> I must congratulate the President!

From his place in the ceremony, Lamon notices the scuffle with Booth. He glances at his Lead Deputy.

Booth is quickly lifted up and carried out.

> WARD HILL LAMON (V.O.)
> *Had I known the blackguard's true*
> *intent...*

Booth is unceremoniously thrown out.

> WARD HILL LAMON (V.O.)
> *...Booth's eyes would have never*
> *again beheld the sun.*

SLO-MO: On the platform, Lincoln steps forward to roaring APPLAUSE, and into a sunbeam.

In this engraving made in 1865, the Lincoln family is watched over protectively by Willie Lincoln and George Washington.

Lincoln and his family
Painted by S.B. Waugh; engraved by William Sartain, c1866,
Mezzotin, Library of Congress.

                    WARD HILL LAMON (V.O.)
          But I thank God we deterred the
          villain that day, and that we
          thereby enabled Mr. Lincoln to
          deliver his speech. For it was not
          an inaugural address. It was a
          farewell. And his words of parting
          shall forever convey his spirit to
          anyone not blessed to know him as
          we did.

                    LINCOLN
          With malice toward none, with
          charity for all, with firmness in
          the right as God gives us to see
          the right...

Mary holds back tears.

                    LINCOLN (CONT'D)
          ...let us strive on to finish the
          work we are in, to bind up the
          nation's wounds, to care for him
          who shall have borne the battle and
          for his widow and his orphan...

Sen. Charles Sumner nods, "Yes."

                    LINCOLN (CONT'D)
          ...to do all which may achieve and
          cherish a just and lasting peace
          among ourselves and with all
          nations.

Lincoln stops. Looks out at the crowd.

Thunderous APPLAUSE! Lincoln glances at Lamon. They share a
proud, satisfied moment that says, "We did it."

125   EXT. WHITE HOUSE - DAY   125

Early morning. Somewhere a rooster CROWS, and a cannon FIRES.
More EXPLOSIONS follow, and the ground shakes.

                    WARD HILL LAMON (V.O.)
          April 10, 1865. We awoke to the
          sound of cannon: a 500 gun salute
          to the President. The war was won.

126   EXT. PENNSYLVANIA AVENUE - NIGHT   126

A massive, illuminated banner proclaims "UNION".

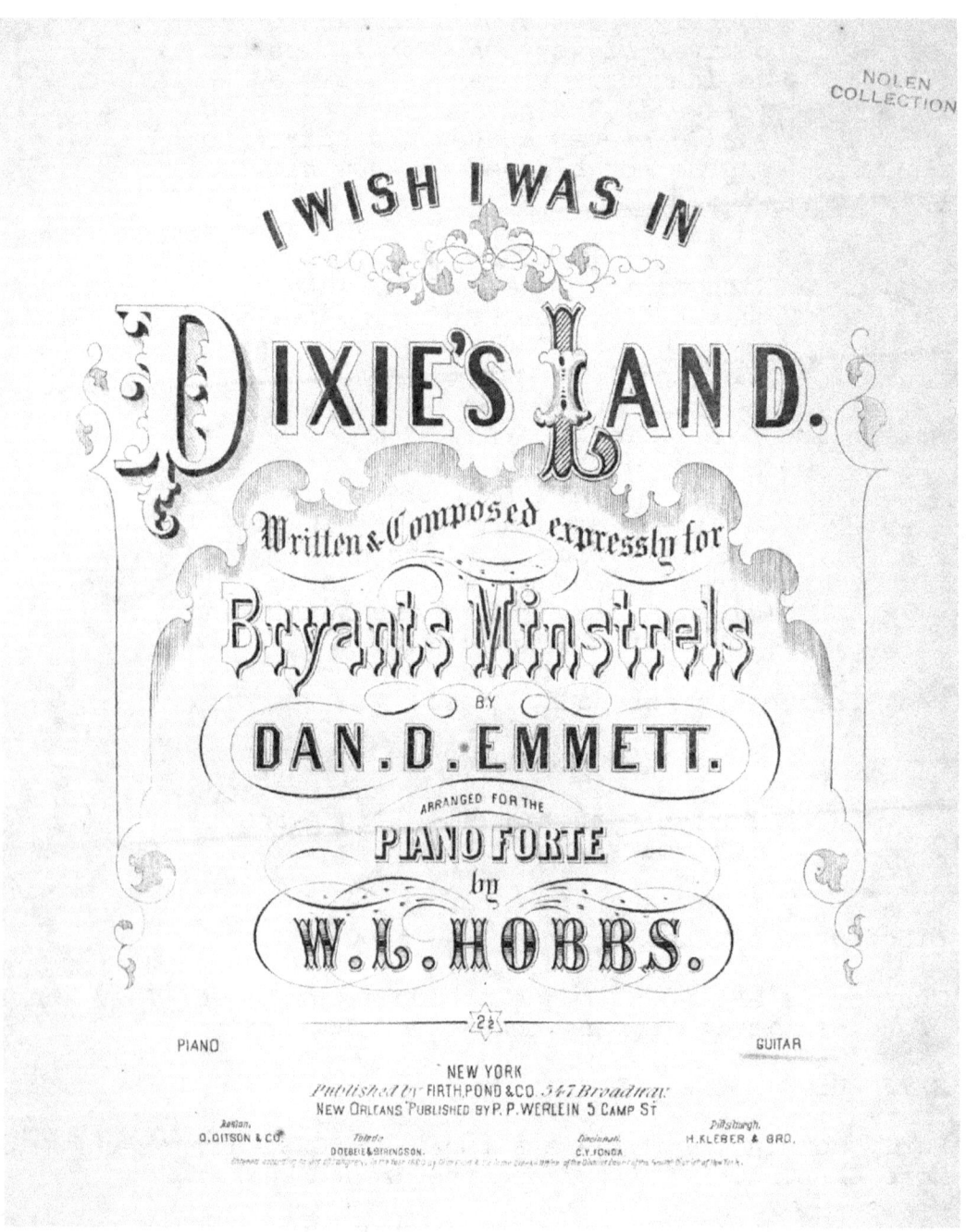

"Dixie," also known as "I Wish I Was in Dixie" and "Dixie's Land," was written by a Northerner, Dan Emmett, sometime in the 1850's. Emmett performed "Dixie" with his blackface troupe, Bryant's Minstrels, in a show that traveled around the country. The song was one of Lincoln's favorites.

On a speaker's platform in front of it, Lamon stands on one side of Lincoln, Mary and Tad on the other. Lincoln puts his arm around Mary.

The MARINE BAND sits nearby. The platform faces a giddy CROWD.

> LINCOLN
> We meet this evening, not in sorrow
> but in gladness of heart!

Great APPLAUSE.

> LINCOLN (CONT'D)
> A call for a national Thanksgiving
> is being prepared, and will be duly
> promulgated...

More APPLAUSE.

> LINCOLN (CONT'D)
> ...but for now, I shall request one
> of the best songs I ever heard.
> Captain, let the band play "Dixie."

Silence falls over the crowd, then GRUMBLING.

> LINCOLN (CONT'D)
> Friends, it's time we returned it
> to the national song-book.

> MAN IN THE CROWD
> Play "Battle Hymn of the Republic!"

> OTHERS
> Yeah, "Battle Hymn!"

The BAND CAPTAIN hesitates.

> CROWD
> This ain't Kentucky, Old Abe! Play
> "Battle Hymn!"

Lamon reaches for his revolver.

And then little Tad steps out in front of his father, and sings:

> TAD
> *I wish I was in the land of cotton,*
> *Old times there are not forgotten!*

Lincoln joins in, and a MARINE FLUTE PLAYER does too.

Lincoln gave Lamon a pass reading, "Allow the bearer, W.H. Lamon and friend with ordinary baggage to pass from Washington to Richmond and return. A. Lincoln, April 11, 1865"

Lamon had a silver box made for the pass and carried in his pocket for the rest of his life. One can only imagine how many times he showed it to people after they learned he was Abraham Lincoln's bodyguard.

Ward Hill Lamon, ca. 1863
Courtesy of the Meserve-Kunhardt Foundation

                    LINCOLN & TAD
Look away! Look away!
Look away, Dixie land!

                    TAD
In Dixie Land, where I was born in,
early on one frosty mornin',

                LINCOLN, TAD & LAMON
Look away, look away.
Look away Dixie Land!
Oh, I wish I was in Dixie,

                    CROWD
Hooray! Hooray!

The Captain finally cues his Band.

                LINCOLN, TAD & LAMON
In Dixie land I'll take my stand,

                    CROWD
To live and die in Dixie!

                    ALL
Away! Away!
Away down south in Dixie!
Away! Away!
Away down south in Dixie!

127   INT. WHITE HOUSE MAIN HALL - NIGHT   127

The celebration continues inside. Lots of MERRY PEOPLE. Still
humming Dixie, Lamon helps himself to some punch.

                    LINCOLN
There you are, old friend.

                WARD HILL LAMON
On such a night, put aside your
temperate ways and have a bumper!

Lamon hands Lincoln a drink. The President raises his glass
merrily, but leaves it undiminished while Lamon drinks.

                    LINCOLN
Hill, I have a mission for you.

                WARD HILL LAMON
Oh?

                    LINCOLN
I need an Ambassador: a Virginian
with tact and diplo-

17th New York Battery, May 1863. The Capitol dome in the distance is nearly complete.

We found this image on the last day of post-production, just as we were building the main title sequence. As amateur sleuths in the Library of Congress, this was a deeply satisfying moment.

17th New York Battery, Washington, DC, 1863
Glass plate negative, wet collodion, Library of Congress.

Detail of same image

Lamon BELCHES.

>   WARD HILL LAMON
>   Beg pardon.

>   LINCOLN
>   -diplomacy to convey a message to
>   Richmond. All that matters now is
>   reconstruction, and I need our best
>   men on the job.

>   WARD HILL LAMON
>   I see why you thought of me but-

>   LINCOLN
>   Hill, you are going.

>   WARD HILL LAMON
>   (suddenly sober)
>   The war is over.

LAMON'S POV: Lincoln nods. A small smile tugs at the deep
creases in Lincoln's face. A smile of peace.

>   LINCOLN
>   Thank God I have lived to see it.
>   And thank you, Hill.

>   WARD HILL LAMON
>   But, you are still in danger.

>   LINCOLN
>   Come, come, the war is done. Now be a
>   good Ambassador and go to Richmond.

>   WARD HILL LAMON
>   But-

>   LINCOLN
>   Hill. You are going.

It sinks in.

>   WARD HILL LAMON
>   Will you promise me one thing?

>   LINCOLN
>   Anything within my power.

>   WARD HILL LAMON
>   Do not go out at night.
>   Particularly to the theater.

What the war did to President Lincoln.

1861

Abraham Lincoln, last portrait in
Springfield, Illinois, 1861
Wikimedia Commons.

1865

Abraham Lincoln, three-quarter
length portrait, Feb. 5, 1865
Glass transparency
Library of Congress.

                    LINCOLN
                (laughing)
          You are a monomaniac on this
          subject. I promise I will do the
          best I can towards it.

                    WARD HILL LAMON
          I shall know it if you don't.

A look of understanding passes between them. Then Lincoln
shakes Lamon's hand warmly.

                    LINCOLN
          Good-bye, Hill, and Godspeed.

                    WARD HILL LAMON
          Good-bye, Lincoln.

                    WARD HILL LAMON (V.O.) (CONT'D)
          That was the last time I ever saw
          my friend.

128   INT. ILLINOIS STATEHOUSE - NIGHT - **FLASH FORWARD**   128

MATCHING CLOSE-UP of Lamon, standing under the funeral canopy.

                    WARD HILL LAMON
                (teary-eyed)
          You asked me why I did not save Mr.
          Lincoln.

Reveal the light of dawn trickling through the Statehouse
windows. Herndon's cane-dagger rises toward Lamon.

                    WARD HILL LAMON (CONT'D)
          I did not save Mr. Lincoln because
          Mr. Lincoln did not wish to be saved.

The dagger hesitates.

                    WARD HILL LAMON (CONT'D)
          He completed his work, and he earned
          his rest.

Swett and Circuit Lawyer bow their heads, but Herndon's
dagger again rises toward Lamon's neck.

                    WARD HILL LAMON (CONT'D)
          Now you will do what you must.

Lamon draws himself up to his full height. Then Herndon
suddenly flips the dagger around and unscrews its end cap.

The dagger's handle is a <u>flask</u>. Herndon offers Lamon a drink.

Ford's Theater, draped after Lincoln's death.

Ford's Theater with guards posted at entrance and crepe draped from windows, April, 1865
Glass plate negative, wet collodion, Library of Congress.

Lamon takes a generous one, then breaks down in tears.

                    WARD HILL LAMON (V.O.)
              How that man loved to laugh.

129   INT. FORD'S THEATER - NIGHT   129

LONG TRACKING SHOT: We are part of an AUDIENCE watching the
comedic play, "Our American Cousin."

Far across the theater, Lincoln sits with Mary in the
Presidential box.

SUPER: GOOD FRIDAY - 1865

                    WARD HILL LAMON (V.O.)
              And low comedy was his favorite.

On stage, an American homespun hero, ASA TRENCHARD, addresses
the aristocratic and British MRS. MOUNTCHESSINGTON, as well
as her unmarried DAUGHTER.

Audience LAUGHS. Even at this distance, we see Lincoln laughs
too. Slowly, camera PUSHES IN, eventually leaving behind the
audience members on our side of the theater.

                    WARD HILL LAMON (V.O.)
              The villain waited for the play's
              biggest laugh to cover the sound of
              his pistol.

Camera pushes past the stage, leaving the Actors behind.

                    WARD HILL LAMON (V.O.)
              He must have thought himself
              clever, but it was that very
              cleverness which enabled Mr.
              Lincoln to leave this world doing
              what he loved most.

Camera continues creeping toward the Presidential box, with
red, white and blue bunting draped over the rail.

Nearer, as Mary grasps Lincoln's arm.

                    MARY
              What will Miss Harris think of me
              hanging on to you so?

                    LINCOLN
                 (caressing Mary's hand)
              She won't think anything about it.

Like so many Civil War era pictures, this image features a blown out sky because the wet collodion process could not capture contrast in bright areas. In creating *Saving Lincoln*, we were always haunted by these glowing skies. To us, they represent the positive aspects of death: peace for the departed and inspiration for the living. As President Lincoln told us at Gettysburg, we must take increased devotion to that cause for which our soldiers gave the last full measure of devotion. Lincoln also gave the last full measure and, like these soldiers, he will not have died in vain if we invest ourselves in the American mission of preserving human liberty.

Cumberland Landing, Federal encampment on Pamunkey River, VA, 1862
Glass plate negative, wet collodion, Library of Congress.

Nearer still, as Lincoln grins, anticipating the punch-line
on the stage:

                    ASA TRENCHARD (O.S.)
               "Don't know the manners of good
               society, eh?"

Lincoln's face almost fills the screen. A shaft of light
appears behind him as a door opens.

                    ASA TRENCHARD (O.S.) (CONT'D)
               "Well, I guess I know enough to
               turn you inside out, old gal - you
               sockdologizing old man-trap!"

The Audience ROARS with laughter, and no one enjoys the joke
more than Lincoln.

The shaft of light from the open door grows brighter,
wrapping around Lincoln, as he laughs that wonderful,
infectious laugh that endeared him to everyone he ever knew.

                    GLOW   TO WHITE.

President Abraham Lincoln, Feb 9, 1864
Glass plate negative, wet collodion, Library of Congress.

Ward Hill Lamon, ca. 1860
Courtesy of the Meserve-Kunhardt Foundation

Allow the bearer, W. H.
Lamon & friend, with order
any baggage to pass from
Washington to Richmond
and return —

April 11. 1865   A. Lincoln